THIS BOOK BELONGS TO

For additional information, please contact:
A-Girl Studio
P.O. Box 213, Burbank, CA 91503 U.S.A.
www.a-girlstudio.com

ISBN: 978-1-936622-33-7

First paperback edition, 2015

HOT
RODDIN'
TO
HELL

Volume 2
By
Elizabeth Watasin

A-GIRL STUDIO

CHAPTER ONE

Dean dreamed.

Bunny sat in the backseat of Evil Diesel, the gang's hot rod convertible. The filtered light falling from the garage's window did not touch Bunny's platinum blonde hair. But even in shadow, Bunny was beautiful. Dean put down the rag she'd used to clean her hands. She straightened her mechanic's coveralls and slipped into the backseat.

"Never had I seen anything lovelier," Dean said, "that didn't have an engine or motor oil."

"You're doing it all wrong." Fairer Than leaned across Bunny and grinned, Bunny's lipstick on her mouth. "Let me show you how it's done."

"AHHHHH—" Dean yelled, waking up.

If anyone in her father's family compound heard her shriek, no one bothered to check. It was just another day in a vampire *siheyuan*.

Dean jumped out of her coffin and switched on the dial

of her transistor radio, drowning out visions of Fairer Than. She found her dungarees and pulled them on, one leg at a time. After donning a fresh, white tee shirt and tucking it in, she fastened her leather belt with the Mudflap Girl buckle.

"WOW," the deejay declared from the radio. "*Love* is in the air of Little Salem for all you monsters, ghouls, and *things* in between —"

Dean ran a comb through her greased hair, forming the ducktail behind.

"Who might have a beatin' heart, or two, or three — or *just* its memory — you know what I'm talkin' about, all you vampires —"

Dean glanced sharply at the radio while lacing up her motorcycle boots.

"This one's dedicated to the delicious and devilish *Perdita* from your fangy *Danny boy*, for upcoming Sweetheart's Day!"

Da-arling,
let's board —
Shaboom-shaboom —
the ship of love,
ship-ship of love,
our ship of LO —

Dean climbed out her second story window and leapt for below. Her motorcycle sat ready at the curb, and she hopped into the seat. Several bats flapped across the blue sky and fluffy clouds overhead; a beautiful start to a special weekend in the Twilight World. The bike roared to life, and Dean took off down the hill, past the other well-to-do and walled homes for the town center of Little Salem.

As she looped around a road leading to a bridge, a monstrous heap hiding beneath an arch offered a wrapped present to another dripping heap hiding under another arch. Dean crossed the bridge and entered the town's main thoroughfare. A hunchbacked boy handed a flaming girl a flower, both seated atop the marquee of The Moan Theater. A mummy couple in Pharaonic garb walked stiffly hand in hand by Limbs To Go while vampires in dignified dress toasted each other at the tavern window of The Noose.

Dean activated her hellfire injection system. Her bike's tailpipe spewed flames as she roared down Main St.

But her fiery passage could not eclipse the ominous approach of an armored figure in the sky. A black knight in shredded cape and bearing a heart-shaped red box descended, his fearsome mount beating black wings. Lattice shutters flew open, and a ghost woman in tattered veil and crown cast her white-eyed gaze upwards for her suitor.

Love's memory, Dean thought, as she barreled past.

Even in the Twilight World, where dark creatures and magical beings found haven far from the mundane, outside world, love had its day to shine: Sweetheart's Day was nigh!

Dean pulled to a stop before the open garage of Soupy's Gas. Her vampire buddy, Cesar, bent beneath the open hood of Evil Diesel while Burt, the bandaged invisible boy, looked on behind his big sunglasses, dressed in his mechanic's coveralls. After dismounting, Dean strutted in, toothpick in her mouth, and pointed at Cesar and Burt. Danny stood within the garage, his freckled face determined. Like Cesar, he had a broad chest with strong arms, though his curly red hair made an uncooperative duck tail.

"So I'm thinkin'…a big bunch of flowers," he said to

Soupy, whose skinny, aged face remained inscrutable. No one knew whether Soupy, in the mechanic's coveralls and greased hairdo, was a mister or a miz. Therefore, Soupy was only known as Soupy. The ever present bent and unlit cigarette dangled from Soupy's thin, pursed lips.

"Tons of flowers! A huge pile!" Danny said.

"No, man, make it one," Soupy mumbled passed the cigarette. "Be all special, knowwhudImean?"

"Dean." Danny's red brows knit. Danny was part-devil as well as vampire, and his intensity made the small horns at his temples redder. "What do ya think? One flower or a ton?"

Dean held up three fingers. "Try three—one each for I, Love, You." She then approached the coat hooks and brought down her blue work shirt with the embroidered nametag *Dean* stitched on the front pocket.

"*Yeah*," Danny enthused to Soupy. "That's just what I'll do. Dean knows how it's done!"

"'Ey, Dean," Cesar called from beneath the hood. "What are you and Bunny plannin' for Sweetheart's Day?"

"Huh?" Dean shrugged into her work shirt. "Well, uh…"

"'Ey, Dean." Burt pointed a bandaged finger towards the lot. "Here comes yer girl."

Bunny Baker, the seventeen year old daughter of a seventh daughter and good teen witch of Little Salem, walked passed the gas pumps that visibly bubbled hellfire fuel within their glass cylinders, her pointed witch's hat in hand. Sunlight lit her platinum hair, its length curling just off her shoulders. Her locks fell in a wave over one eye. Bunny wore a three-quarter sleeved sweater with a mid-length pencil skirt, and she smiled at Dean.

Dean trotted up.

"Hey, Dean." Bunny wrapped her arms around Dean's neck, smiling.

"Hey," Dean simply said, happy.

They kissed, then parted.

"Have you been in town?" Bunny's hazel eyes were bright and warm. "It's like the love goddess had passed through. Everyone's so excited about Sweetheart's Day."

"That's this weekend, innit?" Dean said, grinning.

"Silly." Bunny laughed. "So what are we doing for Sweetheart's Day?"

"Well, uh," Dean said.

A smooth, low thrum sounded down the road; a powerful engine approached.

"Hell," Danny exclaimed, and he and the others ran outside. A hot rod convertible, licorice-black and cherry red with black lightning streaking along its side, rumbled towards the gas station. Before its toothy grill, two steel fangs protruded from the gleaming bumper. A wolf girl sat atop the red, upholstered back seat, her hair fluttering in the breeze. It was Rorie, a schoolmate of Bunny's. The license plate read: FANG.

The car pulled up at the pump. Lucius sat laconically at the red steering wheel, a second wolf girl in neck scarf and tight sweater seated beside him. The collar popped up on his red baracuta jacket, Lucius's wolf's face bore a goatee and a large curl pulled forwards from his ducktail. He grinned, fanged and rakish.

"Will you look at that." Lucius's head lolled as he regarded the vampires. "If it ain't the undead lookin' mighty—dead. Ladies, I just wanted to show you what real wheels are compared to *that*." His chin indicated Evil Diesel, its dull black side painted with crude orange flames.

"Evil Diesel can outrace the Fang any day, Lucius," Danny exclaimed, running up to the Fang's side with Cesar. Dean followed slowly behind, toothpick between her teeth.

"Evil will *eat* diesel—*mine*, when I leave it behind." The girls in the hot rod giggled at Lucius's matter-of-fact tone.

"You lookin' to race?" Danny yelled.

Lucius leaned out of his car. "Yeah, you?"

"*Yeah?*" Danny and Cesar yelled.

"*Yeah?*" Lucius yelled back.

"Demonic Gates," he then pronounced, sitting back. "The ones to Devil Land, at Drop Dead Bluff. Sweetheart's Day. Me 'n the wolves will be *there*, bats." He looked over to where Bunny stood near the garage and winked.

He roared off, wheels squealing. The spewed exhaust made Danny and Cesar cough. Dean watched the departure, her brow dark.

"Yeah, Demonic Gates?" Danny yelled after the disappearing vehicle. "You tryin' to *scare* us, Lucius?"

"Ain't nothin' gonna drop dead at that bluff but the Fang, dog boy!" Cesar yelled.

Both he and Danny pointed at Dean. "Dean's driving," they said in unison, then ran back to Evil Diesel.

"Huh?" Dean said.

"C'mon! We gotta finish work on Evil Diesel!" Cesar said.

"We'll show them wolves!" Danny joined Cesar in front of their hot rod.

"Wait," Dean said. Bunny stood near the car, her expression tense.

Dean swallowed and walked up.

"Don't do this," Bunny said.

"It's too late." Dean stopped before her. "We gotta race,

and I'm in it."

"Tell them 'no,' Dean."

"I'm the best driver, Bunny!"

"This is dangerous!"

"Which is why I *gotta drive!*"

Bunny stiffened, her gaze stark.

She left.

"Wha—" Dean uttered. Bunny was already a small figure across the road from the gas station. She stepped into a hollow within the Enchanting Forest and disappeared.

"*Hell,*" Dean swore.

❧

Bunny descended into the woods, but the cool cover of trees was little comfort.

"I can't believe this." She picked her way across the forest floor. "I can't believe you'd do this—" She swiveled to face the gas station. "*On Sweetheart's Day, Dean!*"

Something sharp struck her backside.

"EYOW," she cried, and her hands found a blunt arrow, the shaft crumpled from the impact into her posterior. Its fletching was shaped like a heart. Bunny held the arrow up and brandished it. "*Pippita!* I'm not in the mood for this!"

"Dang!" Pippita peeked mischievously from behind a tree, part of her flipped hairdo and the devil's horn at her temple, appearing. She hopped out, bearing a bow and a quiver. She wore little, white costume wings with her sheath dress. "How'd ya know it was me?"

Bunny looked down at her compactly built friend. Pippita's pointed tail curled as if anticipating more troublemaking. "Because only a bad li'l red demon would go around impersonating a godling of love." She turned away and resumed her walk through the forest.

"A godling?" Pippita scoffed, following. "I thought it was a goblin." She came abreast and gazed slyly. "Sooo. What's with the yelling? Another fight with your greaser girlfriend?"

"No." Bunny held her hat and ignored Pippita, but she couldn't help the forlornness overcoming her anger.

"It's a biggie this time, innit?" Pippita skipped beside her. "Too bad Blanchet took off to visit that university. She ain't here to play peacekeeper. What's it about?"

"Nothing."

"Are ya surrrre?" Pippita cajoled. Bunny descended down another hollow, stepping across soft moss, and Pippita jumped to follow, bow in hand. "Because it seems to me that you and lover girl have been fightin' ever since ya went and kissed that—"

Bunny's lips tightened.

⟿

"Faerie," Danny said.

Dean started from beneath Evil Diesel's hood, wrench on the connector nut that she was loosening on the battery. "W-wh-what?" she uttered.

"I said it *varies*, Dean." Dean looked over to where Danny stood with Burt, who held up an open book. Danny's gaze was solemn. "Them Demonic Gates only open in our dimension on certain days. That's why Lucius picked Sweetheart's Day."

"Says so in the Demonic Almanac." Burt pointed out the page with a bandaged finger.

Dean returned to the battery and resumed disconnecting

it as Danny walked over. "Screws up our day with our sweeties, huh Dean?" Danny said pleasantly. "Say, uh, Dean…about Bunny—"

"What about." Dean concentrated on loosening the second nut on the positive terminal's connector. She could tell without looking that Danny shrugged.

"I dunno. She looked kinda upset." Danny's tone was friendly.

"She'll get over it." Dean leaned more into the car.

"Woo. Heard that." Burt muttered.

"Yeah, sure!" Danny laughed. "You know it, Dean! Who can handle Bunny better than you, huh?"

Let me show you how it's done, Fairer Than said.

Dean hit her head on the hood.

⌛

Fairer Than stood inside a sweets shop.

The ghoul in the striped dress shirt and bow tie at the register stared at Fairer Than as if she were a snorting bull inside his china shop, and perhaps she was. Once she'd entered (noting that no displayed sign said, "No Bare Feet Allowed"), Fairer Than had remained perfectly still in the shop's center. The silent shopkeeper seemed barely mollified.

True, she was tall, broad of shoulders, and could easily knock over the carefully arranged displays with a mere sneeze. The shopkeeper probably sensed that power in her, thanks to Fairer Than's part-dragon nature. Either that, or he was greatly concerned by the well-known capriciousness of faerie kin. But unlike her faerie brethren, Fairer Than liked to think she could be well behaved. For one thing, she'd brought not one sprite or goblin into the shop with her.

Fairer Than ignored the ghoul and looked around.

The crafted sweets on the shelves and inside jars were unlike any she'd known. There were skull-shaped lollipops, colorful little boxes, tins, and soft packages with devils and other entertaining characters, sugared jellies, hard candies, soft sweets wrapped in twisted waxed paper, and boxed chocolates in various shapes and configurations stacked on tables.

She'd always thought of sweets as an indulgence of the well-to-do. The Folk loved their edible pleasures as well, and butter was a sought-after reward. That, and bread soaked in creamy milk. Butter, cream, and bread made her think of a certain platinum-haired witch, and to bury that thought, she recalled sweets of long ago times while dallying with humans. Black treacle toffee fused to glass in bonfires, candied sweetmeats, sugared plums in paper cones, and lemon ices. Through the ages, she'd always liked cakes, especially gingerbread. Her first and only wife, a witch whom Fairer Than had married when in the form of a man, had baked gingerbread. Her wife had also been a wonderful cook.

"Odd," Fairer Than said, thinking of Bunny again. There was a reason why Bunny's family name was Baker. She put thoughts of Bunny away once more and pondered the task at hand.

She was presently inside a sweets shop, for she had seen what an effect sweets seemed to have had on Little Salem's residents of late. Even Goodie Gertie, the most hideous looking witch of the town, had received a box of chocolates (sent by a dutiful nephew). Such gifts, when exchanged, inspired gestures of affection—the sudden blooming of intimacy and romance. Fairer Than could not tell if the heady delirium seizing the town was due to a love goddess's passage, leaving hearts and minds stirred in her wake, or were perhaps the effects of enchanted candy.

And perhaps such widespread delirium was why she continued to think of Bunny, long after that time when Fairer Than would have moved on to fresh conquests.

Fairer Than picked up a cellophane-wrapped parcel shut with a golden twist. Within lay tiny candy hearts. Words were imprinted on the hearts, and Fairer Than held the parcel up to the light to read them.

She was so intent on discerning the possible incantation, she ignored the sound of the entryway's bell as the door opened.

⤻

"Will you just—shut up. Just be quiet," Bunny said. Her shortcut through the Enchanting Forest had led her and Pippita to a street lined with shops. Without Blanchet to run interference, Pippita was becoming a persistent nag.

"Yeah? Well, Dean still thinks you have a thing for the faerie. Ain't I right?" Pippita demanded. Bunny stopped before the sweets shop.

"First, it's none of your business," she retorted. "Second, that kiss is old news. Dean knows why I did it…though not before I did it. I was wearing Blanchet's *Repelere* lipstick to repulse Fairer Than, and it should have worked. Third—" Bunny looked at Pippita's aloof face as her friend maintained superiority. "For once, would you just *drop* it."

"Gimme some candy, and maybe I will." Pippita lifted her chin.

Bunny approached the sweets shop, exasperated. As she pushed open the door, the hung bell tinkled. She raised a finger at Pippita.

"And *don't* point that thing at my butt," she ordered, just as Pippita gleefully notched an arrow, the bowstring pulled back.

Bunny stepped into the shop and saw Fairer Than's back, the faerie holding a small bag of candy hearts aloft.

"Oh, Fairer Than." Bunny's heart leapt to her throat.

"Bunny," Fairer Than said, startled. She turned.

Fairer Than hesitated. Bunny looked at the floor. The ragged hem of Fairer Than's deep green kirtle brushed her bare toes. Fairer Than stood more than two feet away, yet Bunny felt the faerie's body heat. If Bunny inhaled — she held her breath, refusing to sniff the air.

"I was…looking at these tiny hearts," Fairer Than said. She held up the bag of candy, and Bunny raised her gaze. "They have words written on them."

"Yes, Fairer Than, that's candy." Bunny cautiously relaxed. Fairer Than was remaining civil, and though she was as beautiful as always — with tumbling red hair, a heavy-lidded, green-eyed gaze, and pouty, sensual mouth — Fairer Than made no attempt to work her charm.

"Are they magic hearts?" Fairer Than queried politely.

"No, Fairer Than, they're only candy."

"Might the chocolates be enchanted, then?"

Bunny looked around the shop, surprised.

"I don't believe any sweets here are, Fairer Than."

"Ah." The annoyed expression Fairer Than sported prompted Bunny to cover her mouth, suppressing a giggle. Fairer Than deposited the treat on a shelf displaying more bagged hearts.

"Why do you think the candy's enchanted?" Bunny asked.

"The town is suffused with the energy of love." Fairer

Than gestured, and Bunny briefly admired the assured motion, like a ruler making a statement about her kingdom. It was a dragon-like gesture. "I only want to know the cause."

"Well, this weekend will be Sweetheart's Day." Bunny picked up the bag of hearts Fairer Than had abandoned and looked at them. The door's bell tinkled, and she idly noted that Pippita might have followed her in. "I think an occasion to celebrate love is enough motivation to make everyone excited."

"True. Love is stimulation. And darkness is attracted to such…activity." Fairer Than's deep and sultry tone held a touch of innuendo. Bunny wondered if Fairer Than's seductive nature would soon assert itself.

"I would say that candy were an aid to such stimulation, Fairer Than," she said, her tone mild. "They're pretty, sweet, and when eaten—"

"Are a pleasure." The corners of Fairer Than's mouth crept up. The predacious grin would have made Bunny step back, but to her surprise, she felt unthreatened.

"Yes." Bunny smiled.

"Erm." Fairer Than put a fist to her mouth and looked aside, as if suppressing a forthcoming comment.

Bunny's smile broadened.

She laughed suddenly, delighted, a sound both of relief and realization. She had nothing to fear from Fairer Than—

Or from herself.

Fairer Than looked at her, startled. "What is it, Bunny?"

Bunny inhaled. She smelled Fairer Than's hot, flowery scent, resinous and creamy, an amber and roses sensation that made her think of hearths she could dwell in. She took Fairer Than's warm hand.

"Here." Bunny placed the bag of hearts in Fairer Than's palm and looked into Fairer Than's eyes, seeing only confusion. No fire flickered behind the green irises.

A display box of Skull Pops sat on a nearby shelf. Bunny picked one for Pippita, who stood within the shop with her short arms folded, impatient. She paid for Fairer Than and Pippita's candy at the register.

"It's about time," Pippita said when Bunny handed her the lollipop.

"Bunny." Bunny turned at Fairer Than's voice. Fairer Than held the bag of hearts, her face perplexed. "Why?"

Bunny moved for the door, but she could not help her rueful smile as she glanced back. "That's for behaving," she said and exited, letting her smile grow.

꘏

Fairer Than stepped outside the sweets shop and watched Bunny walk away.

"Well, you made her feel better," someone below said. Fairer Than looked down at the red female with the large mouth, devil's horns, and slyly assessing expression, as if she were determining Fairer Than's monetary value.

"And you are?" Fairer Than asked.

"I'm Pippita, the red li'l demon and Bunny's best friend," Pippita declared.

"Charmed. I am Fairer Than." She glanced to where Bunny had last been. Bunny had already disappeared down the street. Fairer Than attached the bag of hearts to her golden girdle and began walking. "And is Bunny not feeling well?"

"Not when she's fighting with Dean, she ain't." Pippita strolled beside her, licking her Skull Pop with her forked tongue.

The vampire. Fairer Than's mere presence had the power to wreck relationships. It was part of a dragon's nature. Though the vampire had tossed Fairer Than into The Lady's Lake for kissing Bunny, she was not surprised that resentment remained.

"Hmm," she said.

"And what did Bunny mean about you behavin'?" Pippita asked with her brow raised.

"Hmmm." The corners of Fairer Than's mouth crept up. "Because I would have responded...some things, when eaten, are certainly sweet—

"And a pleasure," she said through her teeth, and fire stirred behind her irises.

⁓

"Oh Danny!" Perdita giggled. "What sharp teeth you got!"

"You taste so good, baby!" Danny said.

Dean heard the two kiss more as she lay on a mechanic's creeper beneath Evil Diesel, working on the oil drain plug with her wrench. She could see both their feet; Perdita's slingback pumps and Danny's steel-toed boots. Danny's boots rocked back on their heels.

"*Woooo,*" he said, and Perdita giggled more.

Dean rolled out from beneath the car.

"Will you take that some place else?" she yelled. "We got a car to get ready!"

Danny looked down, his face covered with lipstick kisses. He held Perdita, the devil girl still in her school sweater and cheerleader's skirt. "Oh, yeah! Sure, Dean!"

Perdita leaned, mischievous. "Oooh, Dean, you're so

faerie."

"W-w-what?" Dean looked up at her, baffled.

"I said, you're so *scary*, Dean," Perdita said.

"Right." Dean slowly rolled back beneath the car. "That's what I thought you said." She worked on the plug again. Oil dumped on her face.

⚓

"So they've been fightin' all the time since you went and kissed Bunny."

Fairer Than ambled in the Enchanting Forest with the little costumed female who claimed to be Bunny's best friend. The sunlight filtering through the canopy dappled their surroundings, and Fairer Than noted the heart-shaped fletchings on the arrows stored in Pippita's quiver. The story Pippita shared certainly had Fairer Than's attention. Pippita crunched the last of her lollipop and tossed the stick.

"I would not hesitate to kiss Bunny again, but I don't want to make her unhappy," Fairer Than said.

"Aw, I don't think it matters." Pippita gestured in dismissal. "You got your foot into the situation, why not stick your whole leg in."

"Truly, little goblin of love?"

Pippita stopped walking. "I'm a *demon*, and this here's a costume."

Fairer Than put a finger to her chin. "I am conflicted." Her gaze narrowed in thought. "If this is indeed a second chance, I must woo Bunny with caution, or else she may reject me again." She retrieved the bag of hearts hung on her girdle. "I shall consult the hearts."

After untwisting the tie and shaking out one heart, she

held the sweet aloft. Pippita stood by her side and pointed a notched arrow playfully around the forest.

"*Dare*," Fairer Than read. She put the sweet to her mouth and smirked. "I shall."

⊷

Dean hunched at the garage's pay phone, an oil stained towel draped around her neck. She clenched the toothpick between her teeth and listened to Bunny's phone ring. Perdita embraced Danny's arm, the two seemingly distracted by something outside.

"Say, uh, Dean," Danny said as he and Perdita continued to look out. "There's this faerie…"

"Shut up." Dean's eyes narrowed. "I'm busy."

"Naw, Dean. You gotta look at this…"

"What? *What*?" Dean cried. "A dairy? A Mary? *Harry*? What are you *saying*?"

She then saw what Danny was looking at.

Fairer Than stood by the gas pumps, hands on her hips. Her heavy girdle of gold medallions and large canine teeth flashed in the sun. Pippita stood by her side, wearing paper wings, and she playfully aimed a notched arrow at Dean.

Dean threw down the towel and approached. If her still heart could beat, it would be thumping hard that second. Fairer Than's curvaceous body massed more than it told. It had taken everything Dean had had—even while enraged—to lift the faerie and toss her into the lake when she caught her kissing Bunny.

She'd learned later that such weight was because Fairer Than was part-dragon.

Dean stood before her and looked her in the eye.

POW

Dean hit the ground, her cheek stinging. When she looked up, Fairer Than stood with one hand idly raised, as if she'd merely tapped Dean with the back of her hand.

"*What* the hell?" Dean cried. Half of her face throbbed.

"A declaration of my ire, sir, or whatever you are — clearly, you are a confused person." Fairer Than looked coolly down, her heavy-lidded gaze disdainful. "You've upset Bunny, and I will not stand for it. If you cannot make her happy, I, Fairer Than, shall."

Dean leapt to her feet. "Bunny's my girl."

Fairer Than smirked. "Not for long."

She gave Dean a parting glance.

"May the best *lover* win." She and Pippita departed.

Dean could only stare, dumbfounded, as Fairer Than crossed the road and disappeared into the woods.

⤚

"*Woo hoo*," Pippita cried as she and Fairer Than descended down the hollow. "I have never seen Dean look that stupid! You know she's a girl, right?"

"I do." Fairer Than came to a stop, hands on her hips. Pippita watched with begrudged admiration as Fairer Than inhaled, chest and bosom rising. Dragon chicks were built like fortresses, in Pippita's estimation. When Fairer Than exhaled, smoke left her nostrils. "I am familiar with cross-dressing, having spent a fair amount of time doing that, and existing as a man, once upon a time. I only said that to rile her." She then retrieved the bag from her gold-ladened girdle and tapped out another candy heart.

"Now that I think it, you do look kinda like a drag queen," Pippita said thoughtfully.

Fairer Than raised both fists and flexed. "I am invigorated! My constant distraction is due to no enchantment, and if it were the aftereffects of a goddess's passage, I welcome such stimulation. Once lost, now found, I believe challenging the vampire is the right way to Bunny's heart!"

"What's the candy say, Samson?"

Fairer Than held the heart up between thumb and forefinger. "*Stud*. Rather crude, but appropriate."

"Listen, Romeo," Pippita said as Fairer Than ate the heart. "It's been fun messin' with Bunny's love life, but how about somethin' in return."

"True, you have been a helpful little love goblin."

"I *told* ya I ain't a gob—"

"Thou art my Cyrano!" Fairer Than opened her arms to Pippita, pleased.

"Yer *what*?"

"Cyrano de Bergerac." The faerie then regarded Pippita with fondness. "I watched a play, then a moving picture, of a long-nosed man well versed in love. He advised another in the pursuit of a woman they mutually desired. Are you in love with Bunny as well?"

"*Hell no*. I don't like her like that, and besides, I don't gotta nose." Pippita looked at the faerie, incensed, who turned away as if in dismissal, her affection cooled.

"Pity," Fairer Than said. "Then your motives are truly mercenary."

Pippita tapped Fairer Than in the abdomen with her bow. The faerie's middle was as solid as a brick wall. "Speakin' about money, how about that gold belt?" she demanded.

"Oh, not that."

"That gold armband?" The jeweled band circled above one of Fairer Than's biceps.

"Oh no."

"Yer pot of gold?"

"Oh, you don't want what's in that."

Pippita's face fell. "*What*, then?" she whined.

Fairer Than held out an open hand above Pippita. "What was unseen," she incanted. Her hand flicked down. "Now seen." A small, heavy bag clinked, dangling from between Fairer Than's fingers.

"*Hot dog*," Pippita exclaimed and reached for the bag. Coins clinked. "Faerie gold! Okay, Charming, what's the routine for gettin' thrice outta my bag? Bury it under an oak—something like that?"

"On the west side of an oak, by light of new moon," Fairer Than bade. "Dig it up before Goddess's full face, and thrice gold will you have in your clawed hands."

"I'm on it!" Pippita took off running, the heavy bag clinking.

"A warning," Fairer Than called. Pippita spun around on the ridge she'd surmounted.

"There's a warning?" she cried.

⌖

Fairer Than held up a finger. Pippita, in her eagerness, would have disappeared over the ridge before receiving her caution. "Open the bag only after you unearth it, or the spell will be broken. Remember, do not look inside the bag!"

Pippita resumed her departure, paper wings fluttering, and descended out of sight. "Yeah-yeah—ya freakin' faerie!"

"Fare thee well, little Cyrano." Fairer Than tapped out another heart from her bag of hearts.

"Don't call me that!" Pippita yelled faintly.

Fairer Than held the heart up to the filtered sunlight. Motes danced.

"*See her,*" she read. She clenched her fist around the heart. "Yes!"

⟿

Dean stood with the phone receiver pressed to her ear, Cesar and Burt kidding around behind her. She heard nothing but the steady ringing of Bunny's phone.

She's not in her room. Bunny was outside the Baker cottage then, doing her chores.

Feeding the chickens, watering the garden. How many times had Dean snuck away from Soupy's in order to surprise Bunny while she was in her garden?

Dean needed to get there before the faerie. She hung up and shrugged out of her stained work shirt. Her white tee was dirty as well, and the guys weren't going to tell her how badly her face looked, with the bruise and the oil stains. She just hoped it didn't look bad enough to scare Bunny.

She stepped out of the garage for her bike.

KKRCH

"*Danny, what the hell?*" Dean shrieked. Danny's white and red hot rod had backed into her motorcycle, twisting the frame beneath his wheels. Danny glanced back, Perdita seated beside him.

"*Oh, man,* Dean, I'm so sorry!"

Dean ran across the lot for the road and the woods beyond.

"Does this mean you don't want your Blood Burger?" Danny called.

Dean descended into the hollow.

"I just gotta see her—gotta see her—and make everything okay—"

Dean ran.

CHAPTER TWO

Bunny flung feed to the chickens, her motions automatic.

She'd watered and weeded the front garden, then the back, and at one point thought she'd heard her phone ring in her bedroom. All her friends knew to communicate by scrying, whether by mirror, crystal ball, or a bowl of water. Only vampires, who couldn't cast reflections, used phones. Aunt Agoosta, laboring in the kitchen, could not confirm she'd heard it ring, and Bunny refrained from running upstairs to phone back. She was still mad at Dean.

You and lover girl have been fightin' ever since ya went and kissed that—

"But that's past. I've apologized and asked, repeatedly, and Dean still says nothing's wrong," Bunny told the chickens.

She watched evening fall closer to night, standing among the clucking hens.

Two small, shovelheads bobbed up and down behind the shrubbery, along with the crumpled points of witches' hats. Bunny recognized the hats. Her wizened aunties,

Hauntette and Weirdette, were marching into the forest, shovels shouldered and apparently up to something.

"Did ye enchant 'em properly?" She heard Weirdette ask.

"'Course I did!" Hauntette's tone was gruff. "They'll dig-dig-dig 'til we order 'em to stop. Have ye the traps?"

"'Course I do! And well oiled they are, too!"

Two shrill peals of laughter echoed in the forest.

Bunny shook out her apron front, the feeding done. She went to the scullery door. She hadn't time to worry about her aunties' antics; it was time to call Soupy's Gas and talk to Dean.

Bunny passed through the kitchen, where Aunt Agoosta hummed and mixed cake dough, and went upstairs to her bedroom. The only one to answer her call to Soupy's was Danny. Bunny hung up and decided to skip dinner. She didn't feel like eating.

❧

Sunlight grew dim as it fell between the trees. Night fell. Dean ran, beating a steady rhythm on the forest floor. Only a minute more, and she'd reach Bunny's.

Her feet gave way, dry leaves flurrying, and Dean plunged into a sudden hole.

When she hit ground in the blackness, teeth snapped shut around her leg.

"ARGH," she screamed.

❧

Hauntette and Weirdette watched the vampire disappear into their freshly dug pit and erupted into high-pitched giggles. More jawed traps snapped and the vampire continued to scream.

"Bunny's vampire achoolly fell in, it did," Hauntette cried.

"That sounds like the bear trap!" Weirdette crowed. "And the wolf trap! And the trap fer fire breathin' lizards!"

"AUGHH," Dean cried.

The aunties scurried out of hiding to the pit's edge, Hauntette keeping up with Weirdette, despite her peg leg. They peered down, Weirdette's eyes bulging.

"Ooo, it's quiet now. Think we killed it?" Weirdette asked.

"Our niece wouldn't like that," Hauntette remarked, her cob pipe jutting from her mouth. She squinted at her sister.

"*Hee-hee-hee-hee!*" they screamed.

When they'd retrieved their enchanted shovels and shouldered them, Hauntette pointed at her own noggin.

"Not too smart, innit?" she said. Weirdette tutted and motioned dismissively.

"Better luck next time for our Bunny dear," she said airily.

The two cackled more and departed for the house.

⚞

Fairer Than parted branches and peered down from her hiding place. The aunties passed by, oblivious, their shovels bobbing. The two marched back to Baker cottage and through its back garden gate.

"Hup-hup-hup," they said. They disappeared into the scullery door.

Fairer Than let go of the branches and regarded the

young faerie women standing behind her.

"Do you two remember what I'd told you?" she asked.

Lightsome Iris cupped her own ear, the other hand on her hip. She turned her head coquettishly, crowned with the flowers of her namesake. "Yes! We've ears, you know, and pretty ones!"

"As long as thou does not breathe fire 'pon us, thou *spawn* of dragons, we'll do as thou bidst," Plumelia said with fear on her pretty brow. Her long, thick hair was as straight as Iris's was curly. Fairer Than rolled her eyes at Plumelia's use of archaic speech. The young faerie had not even been born during the period such patter was the norm.

"Will you not call me that?" Fairer Than exclaimed, and Plumelia drew back in alarm. "And I'll *not* be breathing fire 'pon the likes of you!"

"Oh!" Plumelia seemed ready to stamp her foot and the plumeria blossom in her hair trembled. "Shame!"

Fairer Than parted the branches again and motioned for the faeries to precede her. Iris stepped out from their hiding place and pointed towards the cottage.

"Is that not the cottage of the three witch crones?" Iris asked. "We do not like them. They plant bluebells in their garden."

"Yes," Plumelia said as Iris ran with light feet for the garden's low stonewall. Her tone turned haughty. "All earth is faerie domain. We would bless their soil with our presence if not for the tinkling bluebells, warning the witches of our whereabouts."

"And perhaps you'd also bless their cakes with your whereabouts, Plumelia?" Fairer Than ushered the faerie for where Iris knelt at the wall, resting her elbows atop. Iris was looking towards the kitchen's sill where several cakes stood cooling.

"I never said I liked cake!" Plumelia retorted.

Fairer Than ignored her, her gaze upon the window in the second story. A large crack led up to the sill, made when Fairer Than had impacted the wall with her body. She'd leapt across the garden one night in order to gain footing on the half-timber and wish Bunny a good night. The Baker witches had yet to have someone repair the damage and had not even bothered to glamour it. Shutters and curtains open, Bunny stood within her room, her back to the window as she consulted a book. The night's temperature was light, and Bunny remained dressed in only a sleeveless top and pencil skirt.

"There she is." Fairer Than looked on, delighted, and did not notice Plumelia's resentful glance upwards. Iris joined them.

"We are here to eat cake?" she asked Plumelia.

"No," Fairer Than said, giving the two a stern look. "You're here to help me serenade the witch girl."

"A...'romancing?'" A cool, feminine voice spoke.

A tall faerie woman emerged from the forest. Pale, white of hair and her kirtle ice blue, her head was crowned with spruce. "Thou desires that our little sisters aid thee in thy 'wooing?'"

She came to stand before Fairer Than, her gaze cold. "How mortal," she added.

Fairer Than placed her hands on her hips.

Hildegard was older than Fairer Than, though the elder faerie would never admit that their mutual curiosity with mortals held equal passion.

"You needn't be here, Hildegard, thou frigid daughter of the north," Fairer Than said.

"I must keep an eye on you, dark one. You are a bad

influence 'pon our faerie daughters."

"I would like to see this badness," Plumelia remarked as she and Iris circled the two older faerie.

"Fie. I am going into the garden." Fairer Than turned to do so. "Sing sweetly for me, now," she ordered, pointing back at the younger faerie.

"Give us sweets, and we shall," Plumelia lightly demanded.

Fairer Than returned, her bag of candy hearts in hand. The faeries quickly extended their palms, though Hildegard did so with chin raised and her manner cool. Fairer Than dropped a heart into each palm.

"Here! A candy heart for each of you!" She left them to vault the stonewall.

⁂

The three faerie cradled their treats as Fairer Than leapt.

"Mine says, 'U-R-A-10!'" Plumelia enthused.

Iris giggled. "Mine says, '1-N-ONLY!'"

Hildegard beheld the heart in her hand. "Mine says… 'B-MY-HOTLIPS.'"

She glanced over to where Fairer Than had disappeared over the stonewall, her brow raised. The two younger faerie stared at Hildegarde with wide eyes, then Iris's mischievously narrowed while Plumelia's gaze turned resentful.

"Lucky," Plumelia said coldly, startling Hildegard.

"Hsst!" Fairer Than beckoned from where she stood in the witches' garden, then turned away to regard the lit cottage window above. The faerie ran for the wall.

⁂

Danny had said that Dean had left Soupy's, and since Dean didn't appear at the cottage door, Bunny had to assume her girlfriend had ended up elsewhere. Blanchet, still investigating a prospective university for her witch doctor's degree, had left a magical message on Bunny's vanity mirror. Bunny had mirror-written to Blanchet the moment she'd come home. Receiving no immediate answer, Bunny had taken care of her chores.

When scrying wasn't practical, a "text message," as Blanchet had called it, would do. Sometimes Bunny wished Blanchet didn't use the jargon of the era she'd emigrated from when Blanchet's family had moved to the Twilight World. Such slang was several decades ahead of Bunny's, and when Blanchet talked of the technology she once possessed, Bunny could not follow. At least Blanchet had taken well to scrying and magical messaging despite it not being "digital."

I don't know, Blanchet's message said. *It's a race, and she's Dean.*

She can still change her mind, Bunny wrote on the mirror. The cursive words formed beneath her finger, their letters made of sparkling light. She waited, and apparently Blanchet was still available. Her friend wrote back, the words appearing backwards. A simple spell attached to the mirror automatically flipped the writing around.

Whatever you decide, I'm with you.

Bunny nearly choked, unable to swallow. Leave it to Blanchet to gently suggest what Pippita would have driven into Bunny via an arrow into the heart. Her finger touched the glass.

It'll be okay. I love her.

Blanchet had to go, and after their goodbyes, Bunny

rose from her vanity, her heart heavy. But she set the feeling aside. Nothing more could be done until she saw Dean again. She picked up a large book she'd borrowed from the witches' library, titled *Incantation Strengthening Without Tools Or Aids*, and began studying. She was so intent on losing herself in magical practice that she did not notice the soft tinkle of a bluebell in the garden below.

✍

"Plumelia!" Fairer Than hissed. Plumelia stood frozen as her gown's errant edge touched a bluebell flower. Hildegard smoothly stepped up, easily avoiding the bluebell blossoms, and moved Plumelia's skirt away. Iris danced to Plumelia's side, as if bluebells hadn't the power to touch her, and somehow they didn't. They then all regarded Fairer Than—Hildegard coldly, Iris, with expectation, and Plumelia with reddened cheeks—and waited. Fairer Than listened for an attack from Bunny's aunties. When no dangling horseshoe appeared in the darkness—an iron object the faerie were quite allergic to—she deemed it safe to act.

She directed the three to regard Bunny's window.

✍

"'…And so pass to thy east, and to thy west; to sky, then Earth, and these words do speak," Bunny read. She put the book down and breathed. Then she motioned.

She knew immediately; her focus and energies were off. The gestures were clumsy. Bunny quickly performed the sign for dismissal before her careless spell attempt caused trouble.

"Oh, that was terrible," she berated, and her hand met her forehead, frustrated. If she used her wand for the spell, she'd succeed, but the exercise was about freeform casting, after all. At school, others performed freeform better than she—at least she thought so. Blanchet with thoughtful precision, Becky with rote-like solidity, and Lucius's girlfriend, Rorie, though seemingly reckless thanks to her aggressive wolf nature, with bold effectiveness.

Her aunties had said clumsiness was part of weaning off tools. She doubted that was the true problem. The teachers gave Bunny high points for her deft acuity and power—and perhaps being the daughter of a seventh daughter contributed to such natural ability. Without an aid, however, she felt adrift.

And dangerous.

Potential for highly intuitive and pure execution once she accepts it, one teacher's evaluation to her aunties had said. *Accept what?* Bunny had thought. Whatever the teacher had meant, for the time being, Bunny's freeform work was uneven.

"I wasn't even like this as a baby," she grumbled.

She breathed.

"All right." She raised her hands once more. "Try again."

"*Yoooooour spell*," a richly toned voice sang from the garden, "*has me in a twist—*"

Surprised, Bunny rushed to the window and looked below. Fairer Than gazed up from the garden, her hand beckoning, and three faerie women moved in unison behind her, executing gentle dance moves. Fairer Than sang:

Its potent charm
I can't resist.
Being caught,

I must desist
and come for youuuuuuu—
"*Enchaaaaaantress*," the three faerie women sang, and gestured upwards to Bunny's window.

Bunny smiled, surprised. Fairer Than continued to look up, her grinning mouth parted to sing more, and moved along with the faerie women.

Here I come,
I'll show you mine,
Cast away my faerie guise.
Revealed to you,
I await your sign—

"*Enchaaaaaantress*," the three faerie women sang.

"*Revealed to you*," Fairer Than sang, her brow arched. "*I await your—*"

SPLOOOOSH

Water inundated Fairer Than.

"*Faerie in the garden!*" Hauntette shrieked, aiming an old fireman's hose at Fairer Than's face. The rest of the faerie screamed, running through the bluebells, pumpkins, lettuce and tomato rows, squashes, and zucchinis. Hauntette directed the hose at each one, soaking them. They scrambled over the stonewall and screamed more. Fairer Than fell after them.

"Hee-hee-hee-hee!" Weirdette cackled and furiously worked the water pump.

"Oy, Weirdette! Cut the pressure!" Hauntette hollered, the hose's force sending her into the air. Weirdette ceased pumping, and Hauntette fell down.

⤚⤙

Beyond the reach of the witches' water hose and hidden

by shrubbery, Fairer Than bent over and ejected a stream of water from her mouth. Plumelia wrung her wet hands while Iris wept.

"Oh, we are wet, wet, WET! And not the good sort of wet!" Plumelia wailed. Hildegard dripped beside the two, incensed. Her soaked kirtle clung to her body, outlining her breasts.

"See what misery thou hast brought upon us?" she said in anger at Fairer Than. "Naught came of your foolish mortal game!"

Fairer Than coughed, then grinned. "Oh, I think not. The mortals' book, *How to Date Girls*, says that the family is often hard to impress. Being chased away from the house is a wooing tradition!"

"Fairer Than," Bunny called from the garden.

"Bunny." Fairer Than emerged from the faeries' hiding place. The aunties were no longer present, their hose abandoned, but Fairer Than didn't care if a hidden horseshoe waited. She ran to Bunny.

※

When Aunt Hauntie soaked Fairer Than, Bunny couldn't help bursting out in laughter. She could do nothing to help the poor, scrambling faeries from where she was, so she draped a sweater around her shoulders, clipped on her sweater guard with the two rabbit heads, and descended promptly, grabbing a towel along the way. The screams and Hauntette's yells ceased, and Bunny thought to retrieve one of the cooling cakes in the kitchen window. Aunt Agoosta would forgive the minor theft. Though Hauntette and Weirdette liked to keep their home safe from Other creatures, Agoosta and Bunny thought it best to smooth over such confrontations. Offerings from the kitchen helped, like biscuits, cheese, milk, and bread; they had to coexist with Other-beings in the Twilight World, after all.

While Bunny quickly sliced the cake, Weirdette and Hauntette trooped in, exclaiming loudly at how tuckered out they were from the latest defense of their home. Agoosta scolded them from her spot in the sitting room, watching television, and the two aunties departed the kitchen to confront her there. Bunny slipped out the scullery door into the night air and ignored how muddied her slip-on flats became in the drenched garden. She held the plate of round cake in one hand and a towel in the other.

"Fairer Than," she called, looking towards the forest.

Fairer Than came running from another direction, her wet, red hair and long skirt rippling. Her prompt response made Bunny think of a happy dog—and a very wet one.

"There you are," she said, smiling, and offered the towel to Fairer Than. The faerie stopped short of the stonewall and accepted.

"Why, thank you, Bunny." Fairer Than wiped her dripping face.

Bunny held up the cake. "I also brought you and your friends a—"

"Cake! *Cake!*"

"Oh, buttery-buttery cake!"

The three faeries came from seemingly nowhere, reaching over and around Fairer Than, their wet state apparently forgotten. They snatched the cake slices, leaving the plate empty, and promptly ran off to settle in a patch of grass by the forest's edge.

Bunny glanced at the empty plate she held, with nary a crumb.

"Did you…enjoy my song, Bunny?" Fairer Than said. She held the ends of the towel, then draped around her neck. The corners of Bunny's mouth crept up and she folded her arms.

"I did," she admitted. "But why did you choose that one?"

Fairer Than rested her hands on the wall's top, expectant. "Because it was pretty?"

"It was very provocative, Fairer Than."

"Yes, but aren't all such songs, nowadays? Especially as that one was written by a frog."

Bunny turned away, a hand to her mouth. She could not help her mirth. Fairer Than's jest had been intentional, and it surprised Bunny to witness whimsy from Fairer Than—and delight, as if it pleased her to make Bunny laugh.

"How are you, Bunny?" Fairer Than then asked, her manner gently solicitous. Bunny nearly felt the question held concern. When she glanced over, she saw the three faeries beyond Fairer Than's shoulder, enjoying cake beneath the moonlight. They laughed, happy.

"I'm…fine," Bunny answered, reminded of her recent unhappiness. "Thank you. And you?"

"Oh, very well." Fairer Than grinned. "A pretty night for songs, isn't it?"

Bunny felt her own mouth twist, wry. The wolf in Fairer Than was reemerging. Bunny stepped away, holding her plate.

"Good night, Fairer Than," she bade.

She felt Fairer Than's gaze upon her as she turned for the cottage.

"Good night, Bunny," Fairer Than said.

"Mmm." Fairer Than watched Bunny disappear within the cottage, the door closing behind her. Though Bunny demurely wore a sweater over her simple outfit, Fairer Than appreciated her tiny feminine touches; bunny heads had decorated the sweater guard's clips, and a small, gold triskelion dangled from Bunny's necklace. Fairer Than had a fondness for the symbol.

"A girl to ask out for dewdrops and mist cakes, assuredly," she said with a grin.

"Thou art—*whipped*," Plumelia exclaimed, suddenly by Fairer Than's side, and Iris giggled behind her.

Fairer Than huffed, then collapsed against the stonewall with her head resting against a hand. One reason she eschewed the company of the Daughters of the Court was for their giggly frivolity. Iris knelt and mimicked her.

"Some 'daughter of darkness,'" Plumelia mocked and wiggled her fingers in a spooky fashion. "Acting the weakling *mortal*. You would have seduced the young witch by now with your wily, dragon ways."

"Oh so wily," Iris said.

"Mark, she hath that power still," Hildegard said lightly as she strolled up. "But for the moment...*tamed*."

Plumelia and Iris broke into laughter.

Fairer Than rose, fists clenched. She advanced with a growl.

"*Away* with you," she ordered and stamped her foot. The younger faerie shrieked and did so, fleeing in mock fear, while Hildegard arched a brow and departed after them.

"Hmph." Fairer Than watched them go. Since her kin had been given cake, she was certain the Baker cottage and its witches would no longer be of interest to such troublemakers. She straightened the towel around her neck.

"Damn faerie," she muttered, then heard a loud scrape across the ground. She turned towards the sound.

Dean lurched up to the back gate, dragging one leg locked in a jawed trap. She stopped, pulled her leg out of the trap, and then punted the contraption over the treetops. Disheveled and dirty, she raised her gaze for Bunny's window.

Fairer Than moved to leap over the wall, but Dean moved first. The vampire jumped.

❦

Bunny no longer heard giggling beyond the garden and decided that the faeries—and Fairer Than—had finally left for the night. She took hold of her shutters and closed them.

WHAM

"*Ow!*" she heard behind the shutters.

"Goddess—*Dean?*" she cried and flung her shutters open. One of the doors hit Dean in the face again.

❦

"Ah—hiya, Bunny," Dean said, holding her stinging nose. Her other hand gripped Bunny's cracked sill. Bunny had never explained how the long and large crack happened beneath her window, and Dean thought her impact might have worsened it. She kept her footing on the wall's timber frame and tried to look assured.

"Oh, Dean, I'm so sorry!" Bunny grabbed Dean's face. "And what's this dark bruise on the side of your face? Were you just in a fight?"

"Uh…naw," Dean said, sheepish. The fact that she'd been tapped in the face—by a faerie, no less, even if dragon-enhanced—didn't count as a fight, in her book. "I fell into a hole…and stuff."

Bunny let go and went to her pitcher and basin stand. She poured out water. "I'll make something for it."

"Aw, Bunny, you don't have to," Dean protested. As a vampire, the injury would soon disappear. "I—"

Pok

At the sharp blow, Dean swiveled and saw the tiny missile that had bounced off her head before it fell away into the dark: an acorn.

She looked down. Fairer Than lounged atop the garden wall and waved.

"Why, you—" Dean grated.

Bunny grabbed Dean's face again and brought it around. She pressed a wet, cool cloth to Dean's cheek. It smelled of comfrey.

"It looks like someone hit you," Bunny said. Dean took hold of Bunny's hand and brought it down.

"Bunny, listen…I'm sorry about before. I didn't mean to start a fight."

"I'm sorry too, Dean." Her gaze was sad. "I hate it when we fight."

Dean took Bunny's hand, and Bunny sat down by the cracked wall and windowsill. They held hands for a while.

"Look," Dean finally said. "Let's forget about before, okay? We'll do what you want on Sweetheart's Day."

"Dean, all I want is to be with you."

Dean put her head down on the arm resting on the sill. She couldn't look at Bunny right then.

"Okay," she said.

"Dean." Bunny looked at her. "You're still racing, aren't you."

Dean held her hand and said nothing.

Bunny let go and rose.

"Bunny!" Dean straightened. "I have to! Lucius—"

"Lucius is a troublemaker! I've known him since we were little. He'll do *anything* crazy to impress the girls!" Bunny raised her open hands, entreating. "*Why* are you doing this?"

Dean hesitated. *Why, indeed?*

Her eyes narrowed. "I'll look stupid if I don't."

"'Stupid' is doing something as suicidal as racing through the Demonic Gates," Bunny reasoned.

"And is that as *stupid* as kissing some faerie?" Dean demanded.

The look on Bunny's face—the world seemed flipped, the air torn asunder.

"*Break*," Bunny intoned, her voice stark and faraway. Power lit her hands.

"*Bunny*," Dean shouted. The windowsill and its wall disappeared in her grasp. She held nothing. Her feet slipped and Dean fell into the darkness.

Boom—

When the dust cleared, Dean looked up at Bunny's window and the wall and sill that were no longer there.

"BUNNY!"

"Ha-ha-ha!" Fairer Than laughed, her head thrown back.

"Why, you—" Dean said.

Punt-punt—

Two heads of garlic struck Dean in the face. Hauntette in her nightcap brandished a slingshot from her bedroom window. Weirdette, in curlers, cackled beside her.

"*Wreck* an ol' woman's slumber, will ya?" Hauntette screeched. "Have at thee, varmint!"

"Hee-hee-hee!" Weirdette giggled.

"Argh—" Dean's garlic allergy triggered. "Gar—gar—" She sneezed.

POOF

Dean transformed, her bat-self flapping, and sneezed more. A garlic missile whistled and Dean fluttered out of the way. She sneezed again.

"Aw, hell," she cried as she fled into the night sky. More garlic followed.

"*Hell*," she shouted.

≈

"Ha." Fairer Than leaned back on the stonewall, smug. "The vampire makes it easy."

"*Bunny!*" Hauntette shouted within the house. "If y'friends make a racket the next time they're over here, yer *grrrounded*, d'ye hear, young lady? BUNNY!"

SLAM

A form fled down the garden walk and through the wooden gate. Platinum hair and a draped sweater disappeared into the dark.

Fairer Than paused. She disembarked from the wall.

As she followed the wall to the path leading from the flung open gate, Plumelia and Iris ran, laughing. They danced and twirled as Fairer Than entered the forest. By the light of the moon, she saw where a tiny branch had broken from someone's hasty passage.

She stepped through the trees and came upon a hillside and its lone, stone well. The night sky's stars twinkled. Bunny sat with her face buried in her hands and sobbed, heartbroken.

CHAPTER THREE

Words came to Fairer Than, perhaps from a poem or a
song of a long ago time. She silently approached.

At night
a young girl's
lament may be
heard
for things regretted
and sorely wished
forgotten.

Fairer Than went to her hands and knees and neared
Bunny's hunched back.

Pain
touches
if one has
a heart
to touch.

She held back the hand that had reached out to
Bunny.

Fairer Than withdrew and made her way back across

the grass. She returned to the forest, her brow darkened, and did not see when Bunny paused in her sadness and looked up at the night sky, watching three stars fall.

⌒

Fairer Than thrust aside foliage.

Before her lay Okanee Swamp. She could have traversed the woods, but crossing the swamp was faster. The bat-shaped neon sign of Soupy's Gas shone beyond the tree ridge that lay on the opposite shore, across the swamp's inky waters. Fairer Than jumped in, sinking to her knees. She removed the towel around her neck. She intended to place it on Bunny's porch once her business with the vampire was done.

"Steve—you *jerk!*" she heard shrieked from the forest behind her.

Fairer Than glanced through the foliage's gap. Pippita hopped with fists in the air as a hunchbacked boy in a letter sweater looked at her pleadingly. Pippita's paper wings trembled.

"How dare you break up with me on Sweetheart's Eve," she yelled.

"But Pippita," Steve protested. "I can't help it. I'm—"

"Don't say it! Don't you dare!"

Fairer Than dropped her bag of hearts into the towel and then tied the towel up securely.

"Get out-out-OUT!" Pippita screamed.

"Imma goin'!" Steve ran, and Pippita sobbed.

"Unfortunate," Fairer Than said quietly and she tossed the towel bundle. It sailed across the swamp to land on the opposite shore. "Even little love goblins are unlucky with love."

"You," Pippita exclaimed. She stepped through the underbrush and sniffed away tears. "What'cha doin' in that cold water? Cooling off after Bunny told ya to get lost?"

"Bunny is *weeping* right now, much as you are," Fairer Than said, angry. "And it's all the fault of the vampire."

"Yeah?" Pippita put her fists on her hips. "And you're in the water, why?"

"To go there." Fairer Than indicated with her fingers. Soupy's neon sign flickered. "Where I'll kick the vampire in the dungarees."

"So Bunny's cryin'," Pippita said.

"Yes."

"And yer in the water."

"Yes."

Pippita roared in laughter.

"You find this amusing?" Fairer Than said, looming.

"Yeah, because you don't know why! Man, I didn't think I'd get a laugh so soon after being dumped by Steve." Pippita held up her little arms. "Gimme a lift! I want to see what you do next!"

Fairer Than did so, depositing the demon on her shoulders. Pippita held on as Fairer Than strode into the water, descending with each step.

"You no longer seem upset by your break-up," Fairer Than remarked.

"Aw, Steve was my third sweetie in six days. Kinda hard to snag a boyfriend right before Sweetheart's Day."

"Your relationships have lasted longer than my dalliances." The water reached Fairer Than's waist as she waded. A scaled body lifted out of the black water, curved, then descended.

"Do tell. Or maybe later," Pippita said as a two-headed

water snake wiggled across their path. "I expect that list to be mighty long. By the way, Muscles, beating up Dean ain't going to get you a dally with the Bunny-cake, just so you know."

Fairer Than sank up to her chest. Her brow knit. "True. But it is the only thing I know to do."

"Well, if ye're going to beat up Dean anyhoo, why not set it up all formal-like? Mano y mano! Bunny can't fault ya if you do it within rules."

"I see your point. I will pick a time and place." Fairer Than's spirits lifted. "Truly, thou art a wise little love goblin."

Pippita crowed. "You can call me yer love pixie as long as I make a mint off your bout."

"A mint? Ah, you and money again. You opened your bag of gold early, didn't you," Fairer Than inquired lightly.

"Ya gave me acorns!" Pippita accused. She stood up on Fairer Than's shoulders as Fairer Than immersed deeper.

"I did warn you not to look before the proper time, little Cyrano. However, I can raise the stakes of this fight for you."

"How so, champ?" Pippita climbed to stand on Fairer Than's head.

The water reached Fairer Than's chin. "By challenging the vampire to a duel to the death, of course."

She disappeared beneath the water.

⌐

With the faerie fully immersed, Pippita leapt for a hanging vine and swung for a sunken log by the shore. A towel bundle lay there. She waited, watching the water stir and bubbles pop.

Fairer Than suddenly rose from the swamp, water running down. Pippita looked up at a being emanating heat and with eyes smoldering fire and knew she had herself a sure winner.

"I'm ready," Fairer Than said, her lip curling.

"Aaaand how," Pippita agreed.

≈

Dean stood at the garage's sink with its pin-up calendar hanging above and splashed her face. She thought of Bunny.

"This is not good," she said.

SPLOOOSH

Cold water inundated her from behind. Soupy stood holding the emptied bucket.

"*What the hell?*" Dean cried.

"You gotta race tomorrow. Keep your mind on it," Soupy ordered.

"Soupy's right, Dean." Danny leaned against a stack of tires. He held the Demonic Almanac open. "Ya gotta get over that garlic allergy. Sez here that the run through the Demonic Gates is really hairy." He thumbed more and read, "'Past the gates is Devil Land's lava realm, a resident for level five demons.'"

"I'm fine," Dean said to Soupy.

"You look like crap. Shape up." Soupy flicked a finger and knocked Dean against her temple.

"Hey, uh, ain't those level five demons about fifty feet tall?" Danny asked Cesar.

"Fifty-three," Cesar said.

"Yeahhh." Danny thumbed through more pages. "I can

see why Bunny's upset that Dean's racin'."

Dean pointed at Danny. "Will you—leave Bunny *outta this*? She ain't got no say!"

"Woo," Danny murmured. "Heard tha—"

SPLOOSH

Soupy doused Dean again, soaking her through.

"Keep yer mind on the—" Soupy barked.

"I AM," Dean cried. Cesar and Danny stopped what they were doing and stared at her.

"What are you two lookin' at?" she yelled, and noticed Danny's gaze lay at her chest. Then Danny looked up, as if the garage's ceiling proved more interesting. Dean looked down. Her wet tee shirt outlined her breasts.

Dean kicked Danny, took his work shirt off him, and then kicked him more as she buttoned it on. Cesar danced away, laughing.

"Ow! Dang, Dean, ya got my shirt already!" Danny cried as Dean's boot met his behind again.

After Dean ran a comb through her wet hair, slicking it back, she shut Evil Diesel's hood with finality and slid into the front seat. Toothpick poised between her teeth, she started the car, the engine rumbling to life. Everyone listened to the smooth sound.

"*Yeah*," Danny exclaimed, pumping his fists. "We're gonna beat the were boys!"

"Evil Diesel will slam the Fang!" Cesar said.

"Keep yer mind on it," Soupy muttered, leaning into the car.

"I am," Dean said tersely.

Another engine's low thrum sounded, approaching the station. Dean shut off Evil Diesel and jumped out of the car. The second car's headlights grew brighter.

The Fang rumbled up and stopped at the pumps.

Lucius hit his horn.

"Service!" Lucius yelled. "How about some service!"

Dean strolled to the gas pumps, hands in pockets.

"Heyy, Dean," Lucius drawled. "Ye're all wet." He grinned. "You my date at Drop Dead Bluff?"

"I'll be the one kicking your ass at Drop Dead Bluff," Dean answered.

Lucius rubbed his hands together. "*Coool*. This'll give my ladies a helluva show for Sweetheart's Day. Had Rorie, who's into the *craft*, cast stones for the event. Date's for *sunset*, when the Demonic Gates swing wide open. Bring yer fire retardant."

"Tell your ladies to bring an urn," Dean said. "For your ashes."

Lucius laughed, raucous.

"By the way," he said when he calmed. "No protection spells. Not that you'd use one, but knowin' Bunny, she might sneak one on ya." Lucius leaned back and smiled. "She always had a thing for the bad 'uns. I should know. She's a *great* kisser."

He stepped on the gas and roared away before Dean could say anything.

Dean turned back to the garage, where Danny and Cesar stood watching. The two became aware of something behind them. They quickly parted.

The night sky above Soupy's dropped two stars, their passage flashing. Fairer Than stood between Dean and the garage.

She was soaked, head to toe, her kirtle clinging to her body. Pippita sat on Evil Diesel and chatted with Soupy.

"Vampire," Fairer Than simply said.

"I ain't got time for you," Dean said.

"Interesting, that you should say that." Fairer Than's

tone was ice cold. "You've obviously no time for Bunny, having left her in pain…and sorrow."

Dean felt the night whirl. She bent over, hands at her head.

"Dean!" Cesar hissed behind her. "Get it together! Dean!"

Dean straightened. "You've got *no business* with me and Bunny!" she shouted at Fairer Than.

"I do when I intend to challenge you for her." Fairer Than's gaze narrowed. "A duel. Nightfall on Sweetheart's Day. Choose a weapon."

"Swords," Danny said behind Dean.

Dean swiveled to look at Danny. "What the *hell*?"

Danny shrugged. "It sounded good."

"Swords it is." Fairer Than turned to go.

"I don't fight girls," Dean said. Her tone bit.

Fairer Than turned back. As she neared, Dean felt heat radiating off the faerie. The green eyes held fire. Fairer Than raised a brow.

"Unlike some people," Fairer Than murmured in her low tone. Her gaze dropped to Dean's chest. "I am hardly a 'girl.'"

Dean quickly closed Danny's work shirt. She stormed back to the garage.

"Easier for you to defend a *car* than your beloved?" Fairer Than called.

Dean spun to face her. "You've got a date."

Fairer Than's mouth quirked, cool. "Good." She departed. "Wear something pretty."

The faerie disappeared into the night.

Hours later, after all had gone to their homes and beds, Dean remained at the garage. She sat on a box outside, her back to the wall, and watched the dawn arrive. The sun slowly rose and cast long shadows on the world.

A great drum boomed beyond Soupy's sign and the forest tops. The Goddess's temple had begun celebrations. Sweetheart's Day had arrived.

Dean stared, unseeing, and did not blink the sun's painful brilliance away.

⤚⤙

The Goddess's temple: no one in Little Salem knew what the megaliths had been erected for, or to whom. A notched stone sat atop a capstone to receive the dawn's light, its position aligned with a natural and deep crevice in an altar's stone, lying far across the temple's grounds. When light hit the crevice, mysteries revealed within. For that simple reason, locals decided the spot was a goddess's forgotten, sacred place and celebrated accordingly.

Balloons rose above the temple grounds. Carts with food, drink, and trinkets did business and visitors milled. Couples meandered among the standing stones and children chased each other around them. The drums boomed.

Four muscled ogres held a litter aloft bearing red cushions and a coiffed and gowned Pippita. As they carried her through the crowd, she tossed red paper hearts matching the ones decorating her gold crown.

"WELCOME tah Sweetheart's Day!" she proclaimed, the bangles on her arms jangling. "Bask in the glow of the Love Goddess, you lovers, rogues, and longtime, miserable mates! Ha-ha!"

"And who are you, dawlin'?" a scaly fish man called. A handsome island boy with a crown of flowers and a bone

fishhook amulet draped an arm around him. The fish
man held one of Pippita's flung red hearts.

"Why I'm the Queen of Hearts, of course, ocean boys!"
she said, pointing. "Look at your card!"

The fish man did so. Every card held the same
advertisement:

Fight! Fight! Vampire Vs Faerie For Love!

Illustrating the card was a black bat and a winged pixie.

"A fight for love!" Pippita announced and spread her
arms. "That wily godling, Desire, draws forth *two* foes
for one heart! Come see whose heart will be strongest!
Come see *who* will win love!"

She tossed more hearts and the drums sounded.

BOOM

BOOM

❧

Bunny stood on the site's perimeter and saw Pippita
in her latest costume, riding a litter through the growing
crowd. She hadn't time to figure out what her friend
was up to. The night had dragged her heart across the
ground. But when she'd taken refuge by the covered well
and seen the three stars fall, she had been reminded that
somehow, hope remained.

She'd risen early to attend the Goddess's temple.
She wore a strapless sheath and transparent cardigan of
blushing pink rose—an outfit she would have worn for
Dean as much as for herself and the Goddess. Perhaps by
making her entreaty on sacred soil, she might receive the
help she needed.

"Delilah, please!" Bunny motioned helplessly before
the temple's public magic mirror. The drums boomed. "I

need the sisters' help for this or else Dean—"

"Bunny, for the last time, no!" Delilah was a witch twice Bunny's age, but had already gained leadership of their circle. Right then, her fierce eyes pinned Bunny and her generously lipped mouth tightened in displeasure. Hers was a powerful voice, with a body to match, and in any other situation, Bunny might be cowed. "The realm beyond the Demonic Gates is Devil Land. Once our circle meddles there, we'll be *plagued* beyond our mortal lives."

"I can't do this alone—" Bunny begged.

"So you believe. Despite what has been said about you, *do not* even try," Delilah warned.

"Said—what?" Bunny repeated, confused, but Delilah continued.

"If your girlfriend wants to get herself *killed* chicken-running through the Demonic Gates, that's her problem."

"How can you say that?" Bunny cried.

Delilah raised a finger. "I can, because you are a member of this circle, and anything you do—on your own—in the domain of others will reflect on *all* of us. So swear to me that you will not meddle in the gated realm!"

"I cannot do that!"

"You must, or your actions will come back not only upon you, but upon your aunties as well."

Bunny's chest hollowed.

"Do you understand, Bunny? Even when you act as a solo witch, the devils will not see it that way. So *swear* to me, Bunny." Delilah's gaze broached no dissent.

"I…" Bunny looked away and upon the temple's gaiety. "I swear on my mother's name. I will not meddle with the realm beyond the Demonic Gates."

"I accept your oath, Bunny." Delilah's visage became obscured in smoke. The mirror's surface returned to a simple reflection once more.

"Are you done? I need to use the mirror," an old lady demanded.

Bunny removed her witch's hat and walked away, wanting to weep.

BOOM

BOOM

Bunny stopped. Dean stood by a monolith.

Their gazes met.

CHAPTER FOUR

Dean left the stone she'd been leaning on and neared.
"I…" Dean said.

A dapper pumpkin-head man in bow tie strolled by with
a life-sized marionette girl, her painted face smiling.

"For you." Dean held out a peach to Bunny.

Bunny softly exclaimed, accepting the gift, and Dean
gladdened.

"We'll give this to the Goddess," Bunny quietly said, her
face no longer sad, and took Dean's hand.

The altar for the Goddess was a simple pile of stones,
placed around one with a natural crevice, and morning's
light lit the opening. Dean had heard that if she peered
within at the right time, she might spy the Goddess deep
inside, gazing back. The crevice was draped in flowers
and surrounded by gifts; melting candles dripped down.
Bunny knelt and Dean did as well, facing Bunny. Once
Bunny laid the peach beside the crevice, she took Dean's
hand again.

"On a day like this, honesty's what matters," she said,
her gaze calm.

Dean swallowed.

"I made a mistake kissing Fairer Than," Bunny said.

"I'm sorry it still hurts you."

"No, I—" Dean protested. "I'm over it. I'm sorry."

Bunny turned away.

"I don't think so, Dean. I never gave you the chance to fix things…your way."

Dean felt a specter of Fairer Than rise to sit between them.

"Funny how things work," Bunny continued. "I didn't tell you about Fairer Than to protect you from her. Now you're in this race…perhaps because you should have fought Fairer Than in the first place."

Bunny turned back, solemn. "Don't race because of me. Don't race for me. Because it's not about me, Dean."

"No." The sun beat down, and Dean felt her neck burning. "It's about me."

&

The drums boomed as the sun hit its zenith. More balloons rose in the air, and confetti flew. Two great costumed heaps danced, wearing hats dangling red hearts. Girls in striped stockings and top hats walked by, arms around the other, while an elderly couple, the gentleman also in a top hat, slowly ambled. Dean and Bunny walked, silent and not touching, and Dean knew something was still unsaid…something Bunny perhaps waited for.

Faerie girls ran by, one wearing a crown of iris flowers and the other, a plumeria in her hair. They laughed. Dean stopped walking.

"Even if things had been different, I would have chosen to race anyway, Bunny. It's what I do," she said.

"I know," Bunny said. "I know that now." She looked at the ground, her gaze unseeing. "I just wonder if I can…

if—"

Fear seized Dean. She took hold of Bunny and hugged hard.

"Bunny." Desperation filled her voice. "Please say you'll come to the race. Please—"

Bunny's hands touched Dean's back.

"I will," Bunny answered, and her voice was tight.

<hr>

Whatever you decide, Blanchet had said.

Bunny sat on the hillside overlooking the temple grounds, the great heaps dancing in their costumes. The sun moved for the hills lying west.

Dean slept, laid on her side with her leather jacket doffed and her head in Bunny's lap. The menhir at Bunny's back no longer gave shade with the sun then facing them, but she didn't mind. She was comforted by its rough-faced presence.

She had nearly voiced to Dean what she'd come to understand last night. Blanchet had been right. Dean was Dean; she would race. And for one weak moment, Bunny hadn't been sure if she could be the girl who stayed for a girlfriend's death matches, the girl who accepted the outcome and stood by, supportive…

Stood by and accepted death.

Bunny's hand soothed Dean's back.

Dean didn't need Bunny's doubt anymore than her dissent. And perhaps she didn't need Bunny to believe she could win. Dean only needed her to be there.

I can stay; I just can't let death happen.

Boom

Boom

Love and celebration rose from the temple grounds below. The day was beautiful, and right then, with Dean asleep and Bunny—for the moment—at peace, all seemed well. She would take that bubble of contentment and cherish it. The wind blew.

Bunny started, suddenly aware of two faerie girls who had joined them. One was crowned with iris flowers and enjoying a lollipop while the other, wearing a plumeria blossom in her hair, wrote on Dean's arm with an inked twig:

Field of the Freshly Dead
Meet Mee

The faerie finished the messy, cursive words with a flourish.

"What does that mean?" Bunny demanded. The wind blew more, sending her and the faeries' long hair whipping.

"'Tis a message," the faerie with the twig said, her fingers held up daintily. "From the dragon-spawn." The faerie with the lollipop held out a red card shaped like a heart. Bunny accepted it and read:

Fight! Fight! Vampire Vs Faerie For Love!

The faeries rose and dashed away.

"Wait! Where is Fairer Tha—"

The two laughed as they ran down the hillside, and Bunny crumpled the card, fuming.

"Fates seemed to have deigned you two will fight no matter what I do," Bunny grumbled. She reached behind her to unlatch her triskelion necklace. "But I have to try."

Dean merely sighed when Bunny removed herself and laid Dean down. She placed her necklace around Dean's neck, the gold triskelion resting on Dean's chest. It dazzled, and Bunny shadowed it with her palm, willing

a message into the amulet:
Like heart pressed to heart,
this gold
shall hold
my Love.

"No matter what happens after this…I love you." She touched her lips to Dean's.

Bunny descended the hill as the sun dipped. She entered the Enchanting Forest.

"Fairer Than," she called.

⤳

Dean woke.

She was alone. The festivities below, noisy and colorful, had grown, anticipating the celebrations of the night. Dean rose, jacket in hand, and rubbed the last of sleep from her eyes. She went down to the temple grounds to look for Bunny.

"'Ay! There's Dean!" Danny called. He and Cesar pushed through the crowd. Danny laid a hand on Dean's shoulder.

"Bunny?" Dean said.

"Naw, Dean, it's me, Danny."

"I know that," Dean snapped. "Where's Bunny?"

"Dunno!" Danny pulled on Dean's arm as Cesar led the way to Danny's hot rod. "Lucius and his gang are already at Drop Dead Bluff, and them Demonic Gates are set to swing wide open!"

Dean boarded Danny's hot rod and looked back at the Goddess's temple. Balloons rose above the megaliths. She thought of Bunny as the car sped away.

She should tell Danny to stop the car—go back. Something was scrawled on her arm. *Bunny?* Dean looked at it:

Field of the Freshly Dead
Meet mee
The faerie, she thought.

Her hand came down, smacking the side of Danny's car. "Let's do it!" she shouted.

"*Yeah*," Danny yelled. He activated his hellfire injection system.

Bunny looked above at a hot rod's sudden roar. Spewing hellfire, the white and red car with painted flames sped across the sky.

Danny's hot rod. She had no time for worry. She returned her attention to the forest. There was still one thing she could stop.

"Fairer Than!" she called.

Drop Dead Bluff stood, a flat-topped cliff overlooking a wilderness that stretched to the horizon. No chimney or campfire smoke rose in the woods, nor one rooftop showed. The colossal parts of a demon's stone body lay cracked and overgrown on the forest floor before the bone-white drop; a knee, a limb, and a clawed hand still flexed and reaching. Whether the shattered pieces were of a collapsed statue or of a true giant demon that had been turned to stone, no one knew. Only its immense mouth had refused to drop, the clenched teeth, tusks, and lips floating and frozen before the bluff. Vegetation dangled from the bottom of the levitating relic, and birds circled above it.

Danny brought his hot rod down to land skidding by Evil Diesel, where Soupy and Burt waited. The Fang flanked the vampires' hot rod, ready to race, but its owner and his gang stood away and by the bluff's leading edge, as if they'd been admiring the floating mouth.

"Welcome, bat friends," Lucius hailed. The wind on the barren bluff whipped their clothes. "Welcome to Drop Dead's Mouth of Pazuzu—" He gestured above. "Otherwise known as the Demonic Gates!"

Dean donned her leather jacket, thrust her collar up, and exited Danny's hot rod. Cesar and Danny followed, subdued, their eyes upon Pazuzu's bared teeth.

"Dean, don't look so excited." Lucius cocked his head. "So how's li'l Bunny, my childhood sweetheart? Get enough goodbye kisses?" He grinned, the wind tugging at his hair forelock.

"Shut up, Lucius." Dean stopped before him. "You've never kissed Bunny."

"Now, how do you know that?"

"Gods deigned Bunny would only love same as she, and you're not it," Dean declared.

"Ah, that 'daughter of a seventh daughter' thing. You know Bunny doesn't like to harp about that prophesy, Dean," Lucius chastised. He glanced at Rorie, who raised brows at him. "Rorie would make a great girlfriend for Little Salem's up and coming high witch, don't ya think? Seein' as Rorie's a witch too. And *alive*." His toothy smile broadened. "I never did say it was a willing kiss."

Dean's foot slid forwards and Cesar clapped a hand on her shoulder, holding her back.

"Hey—what's that?" Rorie said, and stepped between Lucius and Dean. She stared at Dean's chest.

"Is she charmed?" Lucius demanded, his gaze suddenly sharp. Rorie leaned and sniffed the triskelion hanging from Dean's neck.

"Naw…it smells of love." Rorie stepped back. "Got Bunny's signature all over it, but it's not for protection. It's a love token."

Dean picked the amulet up and laid it in her palm. The bright gold glinted in the light of the setting sun, its metal warm to the touch. It comforted. She swallowed, knowing she was touching Bunny.

Rorie gestured eagerly to the treetop horizon and the sun sinking behind it.

"It's beginning!" she announced.

⪼

"It's beginning," Bunny said, watching the sun disappear. She'd called for Fairer Than six times, and the faerie had not answered her, despite a thrice calling made twice. Bunny decided not to try for nine. She raised her hands, and they began to glow.

"I summon thee, she of the dark; she of Mother, she of Father, she of flesh, and of fire. Come to me, Fairer Than the Fairest, Fairer Than All of Faer—"

"Hush! Hush-hush-hush!" A tiny sprite in leather pants and steel-toed boots suddenly appeared. Bunny recognized him as one who often accompanied Fairer Than. Mugg's ragged wings fluttered as he held a finger up to his lips, the locks of his mohawk sharp with alarm. "She will not come!" he cautioned.

"And why not?" Bunny demanded. "I want to know

about this challenge—why is it being held in the Field of the Freshly Dead?"

"Oh, that. Tsk!" A smile crinkled Mugg's face. "You know why. But she can't see you. Sword practice, y'know."

"What? Swords?"

"Yes, swords!" Mugg hovered before Bunny's gaze. He ran a finger across his throat. "To take the head of a vampire, of course!"

Bunny's mouth set, grim. "Take me to her."

<hr />

Two pairs of headlights activated, shining across the flat plane of Drop Dead Bluff. The engines of both Evil Diesel and The Fang rumbled, burning, heating, and their kinetic power building. The two gangs stood by and shouted encouragement.

"Ready to face hell?" Lucius called, looking over at Dean.

"Ain't *no* hell like the kind I can make," Dean said, sharp.

Lucius faced his steering wheel, whooping. "*Hell yeah!*"

"On your mark," Rorie cried, her hands up. She stood hundreds of yards away. When she looked westward, all eyes witnessed the last sliver of sunlight wink out. The bluff and Pazuzu's mouth dropped into darkness.

Dean marked where the mouth lay, and kept her gaze on Rorie's raised hands.

KRRRRRRRKKK

Stone crumbled and debris fell as Pazuzu's lips slowly curled. The bottom tusks rose.

RRKKK...

Rorie stood stock-still.

RRKkk—
The mouth burst open, cavernous—
YAAAAAAAAAAAA—
Its jaws filled the sky. Hellfire spewed.

❧

"Why the vampire?" Mugg demanded.
"What?" Bunny uttered.
"When M'lady is the superior choice!" Mugg exclaimed. "In strength, beauty, virility, and possibly brains!"
"I don't have to explain love to you," Bunny said.
She swiveled from Mugg, feeling as well as hearing the erupting bellow of a giant demon. The hairs of her skin stood on end. Birds burst from the treetops as the pure intonation hit and vibrated. She pulled out her wand, twirled it above her head, and dematerialized in a spiral of light.

❧

Rorie dropped her arms.
"GO," she cried.
Tires screeched on the cliff's surface, burning. Evil Diesel and The Fang roared down the bluff, passing Rorie. They headed for the cliff's edge and the gaping mouth of Pazuzu.
YAAAAAAAAAAAA—
Bunny reappeared in a swirl of light, both the vampires and werewolves holding their ears against the deafening sound. Taillights dwindled towards a colossal demonic mouth lashing tongues of hellfire. The gaping mouth grew.

YAAAAAAAAAAAAAA—

The cavernous mouth became a world, greater than the bluff, greater than the sky, filled with the cold light of hell. When the hot rods met the cliff's edge, Dean and Lucius hit their injectors. Hellfire spewed from their tailpipes and the hot rods flew.

YAAAAAAAAAAAAAA—

The teeth and jutting tusks moved to meet. The cars' tailpipe flames flickered before the mouth's inferno. They crossed the threshold and sped deep within, ants inside an abyss. The lips of Pazuzu shut.

And dwindled, the darkness swallowing it. The mouth blipped from sight.

Bunny lowered her hands.

The wind swept through the group, moaning across the bluff.

"Was that supposed to happen?" Rorie said.

⤳

In hell, sound was both deafening and nothing.

Dean drove, unable to hear Evil Diesel's engine, and if not for the car's steady vibration, she would have thought it shut off. The hiss from the flaming tailpipes was all she knew. Towering, demonic giants watched as she sped past—or not speed past. She felt she was hardly moving. Time and movement slowed as if she flew through a miasma. There was no up or down. Eyes watched her from every direction, and she did not know if she were the one who was upside down, sideways, or right side up.

Dean drove on.

CHAPTER FIVE

"Ah, Bunny." Fairer Than held up a candy heart. "I can't believe she chose a car over you." She ate the heart.

She then rested her leather sheath and longsword across her shoulders and walked the fairground. Pippita had succeeded in having vendors and tents erected for the anticipated bout. Females watched from behind the roped barrier circling the Field of the Freshly Dead, denoting the combat space. Fairer Than swaggered, swinging the heavy gold of her girdle. Girls liked a show, after all. She recognized the devil girl with the flip hairdo from the Queer Youth meeting; Fausta, who arched an inviting brow. Feline females stood beside Fausta, also from Queer Youth, with cat faces and brightly colored barrettes in their hair—what did Bunny call the girls? Nix and Pix. They giggled and whispered to each other.

Were her fight of the true battlefield, she would dispatch her enemy in mere seconds—and often sooner than a second. Fairer Than had served in wars and known the horror and agony of men dying on the ground. She took the art of the longsword seriously. But that night her public duel was meant to be a spectacle, and she would try to make it as entertaining as possible.

Fairer Than made her leisurely way across the field to where the gowned and crowned Pippita accepted bets from members of the waiting crowd. Vendors sold refreshments. The audience, the waving flags, the roasting meat, and the freshly turned earth beneath her feet— though she'd a mere bout to take care of, Fairer Than could nearly imagine herself in a tourney once more. All that was missing was the scent of horses and dung.

"Ten onna faerie," a hunched fellow with a surgically sewn brow said to Pippita, and Pippita accepted his and a small devil boy's money.

"My dear Queen of Hearts," Fairer Than addressed, "you have put together an impressive fête."

"Yer big match with Dean is a *perfect* end to Sweetheart's Day," Pippita exclaimed, clutching her money. "The betting pools are hummin'! But now I'm wondering if the guest of honor is even coming." She counted her cash.

"What do you mean?" Fairer Than said, surprised.

"Since Dean got herself into that *stupid* race with the werewolves, it may finish her before she finishes it."

Fairer Than frowned. "Is she not riding her iron chariot through the realm of wee goblin folk, such as yourself?"

Pippita hopped, fists in the air. "How many times I gotta tell ya, I'm a *demon*!" she screeched.

Fairer Than brought her sword down and leaned on the hilt. She suppressed a smirk as Pippita settled down.

"No, ya big lug," Pippita continued. "Dean's racin' her 'iron chariot' through mighty heck itself, beyond the bad breath stench of dreaded Pazuzu's Demonic Gates! We are talking *devil land*, Leander. Can ya see now why the dummy might not make it to our bout?"

Fairer Than's gaze narrowed. "I do. She will surely perish then." She picked up her scabbard and spun on her heel. "I must find Bunny." Anticipation lent her feet speed and her face a smile.

"Wha—*wait*! Come back here!" Pippita yelled.

⤳

Time caught up with Dean, or she with it. One moment she was moving like a swimmer against a gelatinous tide, the next, bursting forth with all the speed she pressed from her acceleration pedal. The roar of her and Lucius's engines hit her ears, echoing in the cavern they flew through. She weaved through the raised hands of towering, sleeping demons, tusked and horned, poised as if to slap down anything that passed before them. Lucius edged ahead of Dean, his engine's noise increasing.

The hands moved. Fingers reached for the cars, like children grasping for toys. Dean swerved and dodged. She came aside Lucius and raced into the next cavern.

⤳

Pippita raced ahead of Fairer Than and leapt for the faerie's bosom. She sat down on it, grabbed the faerie's face, and looked her in the eye.

"Keep yer skirt on!" she yelled.

"There is no reason to remain when the vampire is not coming," Fairer Than said. Pippita pressed, knowing full well she could not stop the faerie even if she had every spectator pile on top of her.

"She *will* be here," Pippita grated. Odds were still against that happening, but her first concern was to keep

Fairer Than present for the betting. "Let's just say I've put a call out to some of my folks to help Dean-o out."

"Did you." Fairer Than's brow arched. She inhaled, as if mustering patience, and Pippita held on, the power of the inhalation nearly popping her off Fairer Than's chest.

"I did," Pippita said, and smoke left Fairer Than's nostrils. "My relations in the fifth realm are kinda difficult, being over fifty feet tall and all, but I'm hoping they'll do me a favor."

"I hope you didn't bet your hard earned money on that, little Cyrano," the faerie said lightly.

❧

CRUMP

Evil Diesel slid through the air after Lucius slammed it with the Fang, sending Dean into the acid waterfall spewing from a giant demon's mouth. The right fender hissed and melted. Dean swiftly righted the car, the tire flaming, and stepped on the gas to get away. Lucius's laughter echoed as he sped ahead, and Dean raced to keep up.

She and Lucius flew out of the cavern of vomiting demons into a vast, black plain of flinty rock and craters. In the gray horizon, a colossal and winged demon lurked, as if trapped or made guardian of the wasteland. The hulking figure turned to watch their passage. A winged head with a gaping mouth of fangs outpaced the cars, in pursuit of a raptor-like creature. Random eyes and mouths opened in the shards of rock as the cars sped above, and tiny arms reached. Dean and Lucius aimed their hot rods high and for their intended halfway marker; a triple-faced demon head with wide mouths containing hellfire. The entity floated, spaceship-like, over the plain, and the hot rods looped around it.

One of the demon faces pursed its lips and blew.

FOOOOOOSH

Dean swung Evil Diesel up as hellfire engulfed.

⌇

Dean's and Lucius's friends were no help whatsoever when Bunny asked them how the two planned to exit hell.

"Well, we plotted a course. Halfway point was the Plain of Desolation." Danny shrugged. "Once they round the marker there, the loop will bring 'em back to the Mouth of Pazuzu."

"The mouth is gone," Bunny said, her gaze pointed.

"Yeah. I should look up why that is in the Demonic Almanac…except I left it at Soupy's." Danny grinned, as if to placate.

Bunny turned to Rorie, who crossed her arms as the wind whipped her hair.

"Lucius," Rorie said defensively, as if that answered everything. Bunny looked to where Pazuzu's mouth had been; only the moon's bright face greeted her. She fought her need to tremble.

This is no time to be afraid. It was also no time to give thought to outcomes that had yet to pass. Bunny shut her eyes and raised her face to the moon. She opened her arms to embrace it and breathed.

When she'd fallen to stillness, focused on her silent entreaty, someone shifted behind her.

"What's Bunny doin'?" she heard Danny whisper.

"Praying," Rorie answered.

Hell was every nightmare.

The nightmare where one plummeted backwards down a hillside, out of control; where unseen things pursued, one street, room, or closed door away; where one became lost, and then more lost, until one's memory and sense of self were gone.

Dean and Lucius were lost in hell.

Their hot rods screamed side-by-side, neck and neck, as they flew over a lake of lava. Giant demons with flat-topped heads and burly bodies seemingly hewn from rock held up the cavern, waist-deep in the bubbling and foul smelling lake.

You could ask for directions, Bunny had once said to Dean, her tone light.

Out of the corner of her eye, Dean caught Lucius's gleeful gaze.

Lucius jerked his steering wheel down. The Fang swerved into Evil Diesel.

Dean spun her wheel hard. She flipped Evil Diesel on its side and arced down and under the Fang's sideways trajectory. Evil Diesel passed beneath the Fang, upside down. Lucius looked wide-eyed towards the lake as he careened. The Fang became a tiny shape below. It sent up a fiery lava wave of white and orange.

Evil Diesel tumbled in the other direction, the force and speed too great for Dean to control. The car slammed into the torso of a great demon holding up the cavern.

SPLORK

The demon's middle exploded, wet like clay. Evil Diesel punched out the demon's back, nose up and its tail slicing the lake. Wake waves rose as Dean pulled on the wheel and slammed her foot down on the accelerator, willing the car to pull free and take off. The nose came down with a splash instead.

"No!" A loud hiss rose as the car burned, lava bubbles bursting. The engine cut and died. Dean turned the ignition.

RrRrRrrrRr—

Evil Diesel's headlights beamed into the cavern, somehow made darker than when Dean and Lucius had entered it. From that darkness, deep and slow laughter echoed. The demons above that'd held the cavern up let go and sank, peering down at the little, melting car. They smiled.

"Gah—" The bottom of Dean's boot hissed and melted when she tried to step more on the accelerator.

"AIN'T—NOOO HELL," the demons intoned. They sank, their chins disappearing. "NOOO HELL…"

Dean tried the hellfire igniter.

"AIN'T NOOO HELL…"

"*That's right,*" Dean cried, and the great demons' eyes were high beams in the darkness. "Ain't no *hell*—like the kind I can make—"

Memories of Fairer Than rose; smirking, confident, sexy, *kissing Bunny*—

"Like the kind I can make—" she said, her voice breaking.

Bunny, who had chosen *Dean*—

"*For myself!*" Dean shouted.

The demons laughed, the sound inundating.

"TOOO BAD…" Evil Diesel's nose rose suddenly, the lights shaking. The hot rod's tail began to sink.

"TOOOO BAD…" Dean grabbed Bunny's triskelion and put it between her teeth. She turned the ignition again.

"You ain't gonna get me!" Dean was hot; too hot. Evil Diesel's headlights beamed straight up and shallowly pierced the dark. "I got something to live for!"

"TOOOOO—"

"I got something!" Dean shouted. The lava rose and whirled around her. "I got—BUN—"

The lava swallowed her.

A circle of sunken demons peered at the spot the car disappeared into. Bubbles slowly grew and popped. Then the surface stirred. The flat top of a demon appeared.

As the being rose, its cheeks bulged.

"SO—

"YOOOU—

"GOT SOMMETHING?"

The demon spat. The partial chassis of Evil Diesel flew from the demon's mouth, Dean pressed back in the seat.

"THEN GOOOO—

"GET IT.

"IF—

"IT'S—"

The car hurtled, ripping apart.

"STILL—"

The velocity tore the seat away. Dean held on to the steering wheel, body flying.

"THERE—"

Blinding light met her.

&

"Uh huh." Pippita knelt before a small demon whose gaping mouth projected a communication from the demonic realm. His mouth's interior swirled as Pippita listened. "Ya don't say," she muttered. "Ya don't say."

"What do they say?" Fairer Than asked. She was entertaining Pix and Nix, Pix hanging off the bicep Fairer Than flexed while Nix squealed.

"They didn't say." Pippita cut communication and handed money to the demon. She pointed at a group of burly demons in leather jackets. Their leader wore narrow silver sunglasses, the glass a mere slit in the frames.

"Hey, youse guys!" Pippita hailed. "Go to Drop Dead Bluff. Get me the vampire named Dean!"

After the leader sketched her a salute, he and his gang boarded a hot rod. They drove off, hit the hellfire injector, and roared for the night sky.

"Kinda hope Bunny will be there to beat 'em up so I don't have to pay 'em," Pippita said, crossing her arms. "But Dean will get the message. She'll come." She glanced over to where Fairer Than hefted both the cat girls, her sword laid aside. "There's no way she'll leave *that* unfinished."

≈

Rorie stood behind Bunny while Bunny supplicated the moon.

Something piqued her werewolf's hearing, and she scanned the black sky. When her fellow wolves did not react, she determined the sensation emanated from the unseen world. Rorie was certain Bunny was aware of the disturbance too, but the witch chose to focus on her praying instead.

That didn't reassure Rorie.

"Did you hear that?" she said, and she wasn't referring to the flatulence Danny had discreetly passed, standing beside her. Hand to her ear, she tensed, ready to fight or flee once the cause showed itself. Bunny did not answer, and Danny shifted, uneasy.

"Uh," he muttered, "that was me —"

"No, *that*," Rorie cried and pointed.

Bunny opened her eyes.

The Mouth of Pazuzu showed itself once more, its presence marring the sky with an odious taint she'd sensed without having to look.

It grinned.

Its lips curled, tusks jutting, and then compressed. A grinding sound issued.

RrrrRRRR —

"Look ou —" Rorie cried.

The mouth erupted, spewing fire and screaming once more. A tiny shape emerged. It neared, a car's melted nose. A figure became visible, dangling above the steering wheel she clutched.

The car hurtled straight for Bunny.

CHAPTER SIX

Rorie watched as Dean's car aimed straight for Bunny and knew—

Dean had told the hell folk what she needed to live for.

And hell liked to fix it where some vampire's love wasn't enough, and *might destroy what meant most*—

Before Rorie could move, Bunny lit up, power spiraling from her hands.

That was when a daughter of a seventh daughter reached deep to beat hell's odds—

For love.

"My plea, Hecate, grant passage—" Bunny intoned, and a dimensional portal whirled opened before her, a massive hole punched into space and time. Dean's car entered it, and Rorie looked up, sensing a simultaneous portal above with Dean and her car frozen in its doorway, then a third portal ahead of it with Dean emerging—as if released from suspended time's grip—

"A triple portal summoning!" Rorie shouted. "That's

impossi—"

WHUMP

Dean and her car smashed into the bluff, all three portals whirling shut. A body sailed above the car's conflagration: Dean. She landed and tumbled. When she plopped to a smoking stop hundreds of yards from the others, her steering wheel was still in her hands.

"Bu—Bun—" she uttered.

Bunny slumped to the ground and Rorie ran to her.

"Hey." She propped Bunny up. The witch's eyelids fluttered, and her eyes rolled back. "Don't pass out." Bunny smelled like only half of herself. Rorie had never witnessed magical burnout before, but the scent of such human weakness seemed to indicate it. "Let's get you a boost from the Earth." She placed Bunny's palm to the ground.

"Hey!" Danny shouted. Rorie looked up. A hulking and horned demon in narrow silver sunglasses, leather jacket, and dungarees shoved Danny aside. The demon strolled up, flanked by other tough-looking demons.

"So…" he said. "Which one of youse is Dean?"

～

Dean stood shakily. Bunny roused in Rorie's arms at the demon's words, her eyes wide. She drew her wand and regained her feet.

"Bunny!" Dean shouted.

Bunny ran at the demons and leapt, the large demon catching her as her wand arced down.

"*Back where you came*," she incanted.

A swirl of magic enveloped them, taking Bunny and the demons away.

"GAH," Dean cried. Demons demanding where she was? She could guess why. She ran for Danny's hot rod.

"Dean," Danny called, but Dean was already in the driver's seat and starting the engine. She sped down the bluff. She hit the hellfire igniter and took off for the sky.

∽

In the Field of the Freshly Dead, the spectators behind the ropes grew restless.

"Fight, fight, fight," they chanted. Fairer Than sat on the ground of combat, sword against her shoulder and chin in her hand, glum.

"Hell has surely destroyed the vampire, and no amount of chanting will bring it back. I want my witch, now," she said, petulant.

"Quit your whinin'." A high chair was set at the fight area's edge. There, Pippita sat, queen-like, surveying. "Are you here to *win* or not? Some *champeen* of love you are!"

Wryness tugged at the corner of Fairer Than's mouth. "Love's champion?" She could not help her tone of incredulity. "I've never been called *that*, Queen of Hearts. You may make an honest lover of me yet."

Something electrified the hairs of her skin. She looked up. A dimension's portal opened above.

Bunny dropped, several demons raining down with her. They hit the earth as Bunny impacted into Fairer Than

"Bunny." Laid flat by the witch she'd caught, Fairer Than stared up, elated, into Bunny's dazed gaze. Bunny fumbled atop, seemingly confused.

"Fair—Fairer Tha—oh—*you*—" Bunny slumped against Fairer Than's bosom.

When Bunny did not move, Fairer Than sat up on her

elbow.

"Sweet Bunny—swooning at the very sight of me!" Fairer Than exclaimed.

"Hey, we want our fight!" a spectator bellowed.

"Yeah, put the witch back!" the four-armed male next to him yelled. "You ain't won her, yet!"

"Where's Dean?" Pippita barked. She hopped down from her perch to confront the fallen demons. Fairer Than rested back and inhaled. Bunny rose and fell on her chest.

"Hm."

Bunny's lightened scent, the paleness of her body's energy to Fairer Than's faerie sight, and her obvious exhaustion, all pointed to magical burnout. What had Bunny been up to? Fairer Than didn't believe Bunny performed more than what countryside witches usually did when it came to spells. She reached for her bag of hearts and retrieved a sweet.

"I've seen you with your gardens and animals," Fairer Than softly said, reading the candy heart she held aloft. "And how you are when speaking to the forest. Earth feeds you. But I can gift you with something stronger." She shut two fingers over the heart, pressing it to her palm.

"*Air*," she intoned. "*Dragon's breath.*" Lips pursed, she blew into her hand, a makeshift trumpet. The breath that passed through emerged as wisps of smoke and flames. Boosting done, she put the heart imprinted with the word, *Love*, to Bunny's lips and fed it to her. "When you wake, you'll feel that even gods could not withstand your power."

BOOM

Something struck the earth beyond the fairground: a crashed hot rod. A figure emerged from the flaming wreck.

Fairer Than held Bunny, her gaze narrowing.

"Ladies, gents, people, and *creatures*—the vampire has

arrived!" Pippita shouted, and the crowd cheered.

❧

Dean pushed through the crowd, her leather jacket smoking. She saw a roped off area and Pippita, shooing away the demons who had shown up at Drop Dead Bluff. They appeared to be carrying something—Dean was certain she saw a girl's legs. Fairer Than sat on the ground, chin in her hand and looking morose. The crowd slapped Dean on her back as she stepped over the rope.

"Where's Bunny?" she demanded.

"And a merry Sweetheart's Night to you, sir." Fairer Than sighed, then rose. She picked up one end of her skirts, rolled it, and tucked it into her girdle. The crowd hooted at the sight of Fairer Than's bared thigh.

"Come," Fairer Than ordered, not looking at Dean, and the deep and commanding tone nearly made Dean stand at attention—much to her ire. Fairer Than tucked up the other side of her skirts. "Take up your sword. The sooner I behead you, the sooner I may see Bunny."

Dean started in surprise.

"Ha-ha-ha!" Dean ejected, hilarity bursting. If she let it, she would laugh until she cried. Fairer Than glanced at her with ire.

"I've been to hell and *back*. You think you're worth my time after all I've been through?" Dean smiled, genuine and wide. "I'm finally getting it, and it's not about *you*."

Fairer Than raised her scabbard, the long, two-handed hilt pointed towards Dean. "No. It's about you. And you forget an important point: I am going to kill you."

Dean clenched her fists. "Not when I got no sword, you don't."

KONK

A straight sword's hilt slammed into the side of Dean's head, and when she blinked the stars away, she saw that Fairer Than had not moved but looked curiously to the side of their battlefield. Familiar voices yelled.

"YUUU YING!" Dean's elder sister Yin, hollered from behind the rope barrier. A figure in black from her long hair to her men's changshan, Yin's dark-browed gaze was fierce. "You need a sword, use mine!"

"You fight your best! Don't make us lose face!" Yi shouted. The eldest sister, she wore the long-sleeved cheongsam of a proper lady, and shook her finger at Dean. Ya, the shorthaired sibling only a little older than Dean and dressed in a form-hugging sheath cheongsam, brandished a threaded needle.

"Don't worry about your head!" Ya cried. "We can sew it back on with needle and thread!"

"Are they your concubines?" Fairer Than inquired.

"No—they're my *sisters*," Dean groaned. Their cries of encouragement followed as she reluctantly picked up Yin's sheathed *jian*.

"Honor the family!" Yi shouted.

"Fight hard or we kill you!" Yin added.

"Hell does not compare to blood kin," Fairer Than said, wry. She drew her longsword from its leather sheath. The large dragon's eye opal embedded in the pommel flickered, and heavy steel slowly revealed. Fairer Than paused.

"What did Bunny think of your jaunt into hell?" she queried.

Dean stiffened and didn't answer.

I just wonder if I can...if...

Dean touched Bunny's triskelion, remembering how

she hadn't wanted Bunny to finish that thought back at the temple, the one that had made Dean's stomach drop like a stone. She hadn't wanted Bunny to decide.

I made the decision for her, anyway.

Dean gripped the triskelion, and Fairer Than smiled as if she knew.

"We begin on even ground, then." Fire lit behind Fairer Than's green irises. "Ready to honor your ancestors?"

"Yeah." Dean shirked her jacket and threw it aside. "But first, I gotta do something important." She held Yin's sheathed sword and took a deep breath.

"*Bunny—I love you,*" she shouted.

Fairer Than started. Face grim, she moved. Dean ran.

"*Bunny!*" Dean yelled. "Can you hear me?"

Fairer Than pursued her around the battleground, the crowd screaming in delight. Dust and earth kicked up as they ran in a circle.

"I love you baby!" Dean bellowed.

⇌

Behind the line of ecstatic spectators, the demon in sunglasses and his cohorts leaned against a hot rod's tail end. In the trunk, Bunny slept.

⇌

"BUNNY," Dean shouted. "I LOVE—"

She drew her sword and swung behind her.

Fairer Than halted and smoothly ducked the swing, then took a step forwards that brought her past Dean. Her sword held in a reverse grip, she punched through, her great blade following.

Whit—

The sword's edge sliced Dean's side, and blood bloomed on her white tee. Dean brought her sword up and down, and Fairer Than blocked it beneath her hilt. She stepped again, past Dean's lowered sword arm, and switched her reverse grip for two hands, flipping her blade up.

Ya screamed, high-pitched, as Yin shouted.

"Yu Ying, watch your *head*!"

Fairer Than swung.

Dean swiftly fell, Fairer Than's blade singing above her crown. As Dean hit the ground, a forelock of her hair scattered in the blade's passage. Fairer Than towered, sword held in outstretched arms, and raised a brow at Dean.

Dean regained her feet.

She ran again, Fairer Than not bothering to pursue. Dean's footfall beat the earth as she made her way across the battlefield. Ahead, her sisters stood, and the crowd roared.

"Get ready, sisters!" Yin shouted. They gestured, summoning martial power.

"Three-Sister—" they intoned. Dean leapt high, feeling the heat of their *qi* build. She brought her sword up and one leg down and extended, aiming for her sisters. She steeled her body—

"*Strike!*" The three struck.

Dean's landing sole exploded off the thrust manifested in three open and striking palms. Her body rocketed back to Fairer Than.

～

Fairer Than watched the vampire hurtle back to her,

an arcing missile with a determined face and a straight
sword's flashing tip pointed for her. The three sisters had
aimed their sibling perfectly.

Fairer Than sidestepped and swung her longsword over
and down.

CHOP

The vampire's sword snapped in two beneath Fairer
Than's blade, the vampire's momentum sending her
spinning and then flopping to the battleground. Dust rose.

"AIEEE! Where's her head!" the sister with the needle
and thread cried.

Dean jerked and her head emerged. She coughed up
dirt.

"Ha. Like a cat," Fairer Than said. The crowd cheered,
and she dropped her sword aside.

"Hoot-hoot-hoot—" they chanted.

❧

Dean wobbled to her feet as Fairer Than approached.
The faerie smirked.

Just like in my dream—

Dean saw red.

With a roar, she rushed for Fairer Than. Her right hook
missed.

Fairer Than's uppercut lightly tapped Dean on the chin,
sending her flying.

Dean regained her feet and came in low and swinging.
She sent rapid-fire fists into Fairer Than's middle. The
faerie merely stood, a brick house.

BAM-BAM-BAM-BAM—

"No fair!" the spectator with four arms shouted. "Cast
iron girdle!"

"Wanna frisk her and find out?" the lava man next to him leered.

Fairer Than laid hands on Dean's shoulders, immobilizing her. Dean held on to the faerie's iron middle, only to be torn away. Suddenly Dean's feet became airborne, Fairer Than swinging Dean around by her tee shirt. Her flying legs knocked down the leering spectators.

Fairer Than threw Dean, low, and sent her skidding across the battlefield. Like a pinball, Dean struck a metal barrier post and loudly rang it.

"Yu Ying!" Yin shouted from the other side of the field, her *qi* energized fist held up. "Use the Plum Fury Fist!"

"The Praying Tiger! The Praying Tiger!" Yi cried, motioning with clawed hands.

"Do the Dead Dog!" Ya suggested, demonstrating.

Dean rose and ripped up the post while a burly mummy man looked on. She held it aloft, dragging rope, and ran screaming for Fairer Than. She leapt.

KONG

The post rang atop Fairer Than's skull and bent in half. Dean abandoned her weapon, ran for the sidelines, and nabbed the mummy man. She flung him at Fairer Than.

KaPOW—

The faerie punched him away.

Dean grabbed more spectators and threw them: a wolf man, a caped vampire, a one-eyed lizard monster, a hunchbacked boy from school in his letter sweater. Fairer Than walloped the flying spectators, sending them aloft. Dean grabbed a gorilla in a sea diver's helmet.

Pippita stood with the wild crowd and wept, watching the faerie punch her ex-boyfriend Steve to the moon.

"This is," she sobbed, "the bestest Sweetheart's Night, ever!"

⚜

"RRRARR—" Dean roared, leaping for Fairer Than once more. The faerie looked as fresh as when the fight started. Dean had a one in a million chance of taking Fairer Than down, but she'd call it a victory if she could simply sink her teeth into the smirking bi—

Fairer Than grabbed Dean out of the air and sent her skidding on her back across the field. The burning track Dean made left a cloud of rising dust in her wake.

Dean rose and rushed back.

Fairer Than snatched her before Dean could land a blow and bowled her down the battleground.

She got up and ran back to Fairer Than again, her gait erratic.

SCCRRRRrrrrrrk—

The last toss sent Dean face-first down the field, cutting a furrow with her face. She pulled her head out of the dirt, huffing. She was a vampire; she didn't need to breathe. But her body was lead, her head spun. She forced her eyes open and ordered her body to get up.

Dean stood and raised her fists as Fairer Than regarded her from across the field.

Dean took a step.

She fell face first.

The crowd erupted.

When Dean's gaze could focus, her cheek to the dirt, she saw Fairer Than's bare feet before her.

"So." Fairer Than's voice spoke far above. "Is this still about you?"

Dean made her mouth move. "No. Is...'bout. Love."

Fairer Than stood, chin raised, seemingly basking in some private realization.

"You have made this a worthy night," she said. She reached down and dragged Dean up by the front of her tee shirt.

"Time to say good night," Fairer Than said as she held Dean up. She readied her free hand as if to strike, and heard the vampire's siblings scream. She knew the gesture implied she was about to punch her way into Dean's chest and take her heart.

If the vampire's heart were truly made up of love for Bunny, then Fairer Than believed she'd already taken it. The vampire was done.

She stared into Dean's eyes.

Then she pulled the vampire near and kissed her.

A hush fell over the watching crowd. Fairer Than put all the dragon's heat and intensity into the kiss that no being she knew could withstand. Dean's eyes rolled back, and when Fairer Than let her go, Dean slumped to the ground, smoke leaving her mouth.

Pippita ran up.

"Two-three-fivesixsev'eight—ye'rrrrrr OUT!" Pippita cried over Dean, pumping her pointing arm up and down.

A large bell dinged. The spectators erupted, and Fairer Than raised her hands, triumphant.

"I have *won*," she cried.

The earth shook as a thunderous boom sounded.

Another explosion—the remains of a hot rod and several of Pippita's demon thugs flew through the air.

Spectators scattered—their noise instantly reduced to the hush of the surprised and furtive. A flaming tire landed and bounced through the smoky haze where a figure stood. Fairer Than peered, and the smoke slowly cleared.

Bunny came into view.

CHAPTER SEVEN

Bunny dreamt, enveloped in fire. When she flew, leathery wings unfurled, stretching for miles. She lit the night with her breath, and when she slept, within deep, dark caverns, her bed was a dune of golden treasures.

Bunny woke, her chest feeling on fire. She did not lie within a cavern or atop gold but inside a very small space smelling of oil rags and hellfire fuel. The fire within her pressurized, becoming a bomb—

BOOM

Her magic expanded at a rate and intensity she'd never known, brilliant and pure. Unlike her depletion at the bluff, *more* power remained, unfettered. Bunny alighted at ground zero of her detonation, the smoking remains of a hot rod crashing around her. The demons who'd tried to kidnap Dean dropped from the sky, and a flaming tire landed and bounced. When the night wind slowly moved the billowing smoke aside, Fairer Than came into view, standing within the Field of the Freshly Dead.

Fairer Than stared, wide-eyed, as if she'd been caught at something.

A figure lay at her feet: Dean.

Bunny's internal fire became a furnace, powerful enough to accelerate a locomotive.

⮿

Once, great grandfather had said to Fairer Than: *the mighty get what they want.*

But for we mighty, he had continued, nostrils smoking, *what doesn't fall to plan is a situation unheard of.*

Therefore, when it happens—

As chance, fate, and perhaps a woman's *wrath may have it—*

Fairer Than eyed a second smoking tire that landed and bounced near as Bunny stared, incensed.

A very mighty person may be at a loss as to what to do.

Fairer Than discreetly nudged the inert vampire with her toe.

"Hie thee, vampire!" she hissed from the side of her mouth. "We need to fight again!"

Dean did not stir.

Alas, no help from that quarter. Bunny exhaled, a smoke stream that held flashes of fire. Her baleful gaze did not lessen.

The plan had been simple, hadn't it? Fairer Than thought anxiously. Beat the vampire, take the witch. No— how was it said? Seduce the witch. No! The book, *How to Date Girls*—specifically said: take the witch to dinner.

"Bunny," Fairer Than said with easy charm. "You are… angry, yet so very lovely, tonight. Would you like to go to dinner?"

"*You.*" Smoke left Bunny's mouth.

Fairer Than pointed at herself.

"Yes…I?" Fairer Than said encouragingly.

Bunny raised her hands, bright with power. She shook, as if quelling a storm within.

"*You*—you-youYOU—"

Light and fire flared around Bunny. Her left hand cast.

"*Hokey smokes*, she's gonna—" Pippita yelled.

Fairer Than and Pippita scurried as white energy shot from Bunny's hand, a jagged shaft that arced past them and into the forest. Bunny's right hand rose, shaking with crackling power. She flung the hand out—

SCHRACCK—

The second blast plowed through retreating spectators, flinging them into the air.

Bunny stood, electrified, the golden specter of a winged dragon rising from her.

⟫

"Holy *frijoles*, how did Bunny get that much mojo?" Pippita yelled. She ran with Fairer Than for the forest. Bunny detonated again, shaking the Field of the Freshly Dead. Leaves rained.

"My error—" Fairer Than loped easily by Pippita's side as the demon scrambled. "Bunny was spent—I gave her a puff of dragon's breath."

"A puff of—?"

Pippita leaped for Fairer Than's chest. She grabbed Fairer Than by the shoulders, hard enough to pull the faerie forwards.

"Say son, did ya leave yer brains in your other bra cup?" she cried. "You don't give dragon puffs to a child of a *seventh* child!"

"What?" Fairer Than's jog slowed as Pippita stared into her eyes.

"You heard me! You've been breathin' on one of the *gifted* ones! Okay, Bunny and her family never make it a big deal—I don't think she puts stock in the story about herself—but it's been foretold! She may be a young'un now, but one day when she's fully grown, she'll easily kick your patootie from here to Luigi's with *pure* Bun-power, and how!"

The forest trembled as light pierced the night from Bunny's direction. Fairer Than stopped and turned towards it, staring in wonderment.

"Why'd you stop running?" Pippita held on to Fairer Than's neck.

Fairer Than ran back down the forest path for Bunny's bursts of fire.

"Ya nutty—" Pippita yelled.

She hopped off the faerie and watched her go.

⁓

Ya and Yi exclaimed and kept to their feet as they watched Bunny's detonation shake the earth and light the night sky. Debris fell, and Ya popped open her brightly painted parasol. A tent uprooted and billowed into the air. Bunny gestured and the tent exploded.

"There! The shape of the dragon again!" Ya pointed to the spectral energy rising among the fluttering tent pieces.

"*Big* power display. Too bad she's not a vampire," Yi said, her tone critical. She snapped her fan open and fanned herself.

Yin knelt by Dean's body and sighed, wishing Yi was

fanning their sister instead, who lay as stiff as a ten-day old corpse. Shaking and slapping Dean had not revived her. However, their fallen sister had to wake at some point.

"Yi, come read Yu Ying's *qi*. See if that dragon's fire is still in her."

"I am busy," Yi muttered, standing on her toes. She was spying where Bunny might be. A group of spectators were attempting to collapse a tent on the witch. "I think the witch will not run out of power before morning."

"What will happen to Little Salem then?" Ya casually asked. She sucked on the straw of her Blood Soda. When the tent exploded, she moved her parasol to ward off the flaming tent tatters that pelted.

Yin plucked the cup of soda and ice cubes from Ya's hand, removed the top, and poured it on Dean's face.

"B-Bu-Bunny!" Dean sputtered, jerking awake.

"Oh, good. The dragon did not burn up your brain." Yin's tone was flat. She reached over as Dean tried to sit up, grabbed Dean's head, and directed Dean's gaze at Bunny. Demons were rushing the witch, only to be knocked down like bowling pins before her arcing fire.

"Wha' the—how did—Bunny?" Dean said, incredulous.

"Go there now," Yi ordered. "She's really pissed you lost."

"She's going to be like that allll night if you don't stop her," Ya said airily, twirling her parasol.

"And she wants you to replace my sword, too," Yin added.

The sisters pulled Dean to her wobbly feet and shoved her towards Bunny. She staggered across the field to where the witch lit the night.

"Bunny," Dean called.

Bunny was a sun storm. Every erupting flare that left her hands did not lessen the dynamo within or reduce a passionate wildness that enveloped, becoming her new magnetic field. Hers was a dragon's ferocity combined with a girl's fury. She could no more stop the ejection of such power than reduce herself back to the sidelined girl meant only to listen and understand while senseless girlfriends ran off to hell — to be *patient* with thick-headed dragon women, to be *discounted* —

A gang of demons attacked, leaping swiftly and with the intention to pile on and smother her. Her cannon-blast flattened the demons. They were wheat, mowed down.

She wanted to say, *I tried to stop the fighting!* She wanted to speak calmly. But dragon-fire shook her, demanding to speak instead.

Something sounded from the field. Bunny turned. Her hand led first. Energy leapt from her fingers. The fiery lightning struck and lit Dean up in the field. Her girlfriend hit the dirt, accordion-like, and lay still.

"*Dean!*" Bunny shrieked.

"Bunny," someone called from the forest. Bunny swiveled. Fairer Than stood in the foliage, a hand raised.

"Fairer — THAN —" Bunny raged. *Who else* could have given her this terrible —

The dragon-fire expanded within her again.

Once, Fairer Than had given dragon's breath to her first and only wife to face raiders, and though she reveled in her wife's augmented power, Brienne had not wanted to repeat the experience. Fairer Than looked upon Bunny, the witch's hair white-light and her face become thunderous, and watched the fiery specter of the dragon rise from Bunny's form.

"Magnific—" Fairer Than whispered.

The blast that hit her drove as hard as when great grandfather had struck her with his tail.

Fairer Than flew back through lashing foliage and trees until she furrowed ground, her face scraping. When she came to a stop, a tree she'd hit uprooted. With a great crack, it tumbled down atop her head.

WHUMP

In the distance, another explosion from Bunny sounded.

"So," Pippita said, somewhere above Fairer Than. "Now you've *really* fallen for her, huh?"

Fairer Than pushed up from the ground, the tree's trunk rolling down her back. She spat out dirt.

"A subtler approach is needed," she gasped and looked to where Bunny's fiery light danced between the trees.

"What we *need* is for you to stop the romancing and *stop* the mini-goddess over there." Pippita's face bore ill tolerance. "And before we're all kaput, along with Little Salem."

Fairer Than heaved herself to her feet, and the tree thudded aside. She grabbed up Pippita and stared into her eyes.

"Cyrano—thou hast truly been a stalwart companion. When thou is destroyed along with thy wicked town, I will always remember thee." She dropped Pippita and jogged away, lightened.

"*Fine*," Pippita screeched, fists in the air. "Go woo! And I hope she *fries ya*, ya frickin' faerie!"

Fairer Than ran back to Bunny.

The night had become pulsating blacks, blues, oranges, and yellows to Bunny's gaze. How had Blanchet described such vision once, when she'd been studying the biology of the snake people? *Infrared vision.* Right then, Bunny was a witch with a dragon's *sight.*

She knew where others hid—in the treetops, behind bushes, and behind trees. Their blood-pumping heat read as bright auras against the cooler tones of night and foliage. Had she a dragon's physiology, she might want to devour those hiding. Was this how Fairer Than felt when her lip curled into one of her infuriating, predacious grins?

Bunny drew breath, tamping down the power within. It took great concentration to refrain from exploding or shooting. Her last outburst, done out of distemper—she fervently hoped she hadn't harmed Fairer Than. Fists shaking from the effort, she walked into the forest.

"Her eyes!" someone whispered in fright from the bushes, and orange and yellow auras emerged from their hiding places and ran.

"Fairer Than," Bunny yelled. She wanted to call out and ask if Fairer Than was okay, but a greater part of her— gone chaotic as a sun's surface—wanted to blast earth and sky again. She noticed that her glowing body cast light into the dark woods, and perhaps her eyes were torches too; she was a living lantern. Nix and Pix huddled, hot yellow auras in the treetops, their eyes squeezed shut and ears flattened as Bunny passed beneath the cat girls.

"*Fairer Than,*" Bunny shouted.

Someone dropped down on to her back, a heavy weight that embraced her tightly. Bunny shrieked. She shook from capping the power that nearly erupted. If Nix and Pix had jumped her, she didn't want to hurt them. But the arms that circled were strong—*familiar*—and the scent of the person was that of amber and—

"Goddess, *Fairer Than!*" Bunny yelled. Fire flared.

Fairer Than held on despite the ferocity of heat and light. More orange and yellow auras fled deeper into the forest. Any second, Bunny might set the woods on fire—

"Fairer Than, let me go!" Bunny demanded. "Let me—"

"Bunny, now's your chance. Within you is that dragon's puff, still," Fairer Than urged at her ear. "Find it, Bunny. Find that breath of sun, and exhale."

Bunny grasped Fairer Than's arms with shaking fingers and drew breath.

I call upon the dragon. Go.

Bunny exhaled. The bright sun within left her chest, exited her lips, and unfurled into the night air, the aspect of a fiery dragon. It rose to the treetops and moon above, then dissipated.

Bunny's legs collapsed beneath her.

⁓

"Feel better?" Fairer Than asked.

The night's appearance had returned to normality. It was dark and cool—the night's bluing of greens and browns—and Bunny neither heard nor saw the others who remained in the forest. Fairer Than knelt before Bunny in the moonlight, her expression soft. Bunny lay against the tree trunk Fairer Than had propped her against, the earth and grass beneath her hands. Her arms were limp pasta. She was as feeble as a newborn.

"I'm still mad at you," Bunny said.

"I did not kill her, Bunny," Fairer Than gently said.

"And you called Dean out to the Field of the Freshly Dead for what, then? A friendly conversation?"

"You have me," Fairer Than admitted. "It was a challenge of a darker nature. But I only intended to give the love goblin her spectacle. Nothing more."

"Pippita," Bunny groaned.

"Indeed." Fairer Than gazed, tender.

"The fight's done," Fairer Than then said, "to everyone's satisfaction. Sweetheart's Night draws to its close. Won't you go out with me, Bunny?"

Bunny stilled.

"I love Dean, Fairer Than," she said.

"I know that." Fairer Than's tone was calm and matter-of-fact, as if Bunny had said she loved ice cream.

"Fighting...one fight does not make me forget her." Bunny searched for comprehension in Fairer Than's gaze. "I'm not leaving Dean, Fairer Than."

Fairer Than's gaze slid, oblique. She rose, walked away, and leaned a forearm upon a tree. Bunny looked at her back.

"She did leave you for a car," Fairer Than stated.

The observation stabbed. Bunny jerked in response — the pain still fresh in her heart. She did not think Fairer Than meant ill; she was only voicing fact.

"I know," Bunny said softly. "We've talked about that."

⊰⊱

Fairer Than turned back and spied Bunny's pain.

Her own brow suddenly mirrored Bunny's, a foreign expression. She stepped forwards, prompted by the same odd desire that had wanted her to touch Bunny by the covered well.

"I have seen you unhappy," Fairer Than said. "Though I'm guilty of also causing grief—for I know my limits. I cannot boast of being smarter, kinder, or less callous than the vampire—I cannot bear seeing unhappiness in you."

She knelt before Bunny once more, hands to the ground.

"You can do no worse with me," she said.

"I still love Dean, Fairer Than." Bunny's quiet tone was firm.

"And if the vampire had never been and I had been first to woo you?"

"I'm not going to answer that."

"Then I had a chance."

"Fairer Than, don't," Bunny ordered.

"Bunny..." Fairer Than leaned closer. Conviction possessed her. "This is more than that notch in my belt that you'd spoken of."

Bunny's gaze held a swift parade of emotions, and Fairer Than pressed.

"You are a value beyond mere pleasure, curiosity, or conquest," she said, earnest. "Or convenience. I am taken with you. I believe...I believe you are in my heart." Fairer Than placed her hand over the spot. "All I possess there is its mere shadow, a poor substitute. How you've impressed upon that dark space! And had I understood this before, I would have valued you more. I do value you. I should have killed the vampire when I had the chance."

Bunny's eyes widened, and Fairer Than did not know what that meant.

Then Bunny's gaze narrowed. "Fairer Than. Help me up."

Fairer Than did, Bunny gripping her forearms as she held Bunny by the waist. Obviously drained, Bunny needed to lean against the tree. Fairer Than wanted to tell her: your light rose dress, it becomes you. Your perfume, it befits. Instead, Fairer Than leaned closer to Bunny's lips.

Bunny's wand pressed against the side of Fairer Than's face.

"You are a cad." Bunny moved Fairer Than's face away with her wand. "An infuriating, bull-headed cad. But you're honest, and I thank you for that."

"Bunny—"

Bunny held her wand before her in warning, and Fairer Than understood. She stepped back. Bunny steadied herself against the tree.

"As long as you're a threat to Dean, we can't even be friends!" Bunny ejected. "I know it's your nature to be so—*dominating*, so I'll forgive you this once."

"Bunny, the vampire does not deserve you." Fairer Than's tone broached no dissent.

"It's not about who deserves who," Bunny said, firm. "It's about love. I'll say this in a way you can understand. Fight me."

"What?"

"Fight me. Let's go." Bunny held her wand up, determined. "You win, you can have me."

"Don't be absurd!" Fairer Than snapped. "I do not fight—"

She stopped.

"I do not fight girls," she said.

⤳

Fairer Than turned away, but Bunny held the tree behind her and kept her wand to the fore. When Fairer Than looked askance at her, her green eye wide and glittering, Bunny stared into its depth and searched.

There — the darkness Fairer Than harbored. One Bunny now knew. Its memory still burned inside her chest. It was the firestorm within that could become destruction.

Bunny kept her wand up and waited. No breath or wind sounded.

Fairer Than dropped to a knee on the forest floor and genuflected. Bowed thus before Bunny, she opened her arms.

"As my lady wishes," she said, her voice a knell. "Do to me what you should have done…upon our first meeting."

Bunny met Fairer Than's dark gaze. No fire roiled. Her eyes were black hearths.

"*Beat it, dematerialize*," Bunny whispered. Her wand came down.

⚮

Light sparkled before Fairer Than's eyes, the manifestation of a good witch's white magic. Bunny and the forest disappeared, and then Fairer Than viewed the sky. The moon looked down upon her. She dropped back, a great stone, her body arcing. She fell head down for the black waters of The Lady's Lake. When she hit, the freezing water thundered.

⚮

Bunny lay on the forest floor, her spell to send Fairer Than to the lake nearly causing her to pass out. And perhaps she also lay from the burden of having broken someone's heart.

"Not now," she murmured.

She dragged herself up to her elbows, then her knees. She gained her feet, wand clenched. The step she took was shaky. Determined, she took another. She headed for the Field of the Freshly Dead.

"I," she said, "have a girlfriend to take care of."

She wiped at tears and kept her feet moving.

⟲

Yin poured a cup of water over Dean's head. Dean did not stir, and the ground was becoming mud beneath her.

"Acupuncture is not working either," Ya said as she knelt next to Yin, her sewing needle poking Dean in the leg.

"I think she's really dead this time," Yi declared above them. She turned to leave, and the remaining sisters rose to follow.

"What do we tell Pop?" Yin asked as they walked off the field.

"Not sure," Yi said and snapped her fan shut. "Are you ready to become number one son?"

They disappeared into the forest fog that had gathered. In the field, Dean lay as dead.

Her mouth dropped open.

An exhalation left, the smoke forming the shape of a tiny dragon. It rose into the air and fragmented. Dean jerked awake, and her body loudly snapped.

"OW," she cried. "B-Bunny?"

When she tried to get up, her body cracked more.

"*Augh.*" She felt as if she'd been fried and then fused into brittle glass.

"W-where's—?" Neck popping, she looked around as the cold wind blew.

The littered and churned up earth of the field was

deserted, the collapsed tents flapping. A smoking tire lay in the distance, and ground fog slowly rolled in.

"Gotta find—" Dean crawled, her body loudly protesting. "Gotta find her."

"Dean?" Bunny called. She emerged from fog and the forest edge.

"Oh, Goddess," Dean ejected, and her heart yearned to fly to Bunny. Bunny looked as spent as Dean felt, yet more beautiful than ever.

Dean rose to her feet despite her cracking bones and stumbled across the wide field. Bunny's own steps were ungainly as she moved to meet her. Whatever had happened after Fairer Than had kissed Dean...somehow, Bunny was the last woman standing.

Dean wanted to weep.

"Some Sweetheart's Night, huh?" she called cheerfully. Her boots nearly gave way beneath her. Bunny's face lit, exasperated.

"Oh, you—get over here!" Bunny demanded.

They met in the middle of the field, Bunny pulling Dean into her arms. Dean felt she'd found home.

"Wait." She pulled back. She held Bunny away and steeled herself. "I've been wanting to say this to you, all night." Dean fell to her knees and hung her head. "I don't deserve you, Bunny!"

"*Goddess*, not you too?" Bunny cried.

Dean looked up. "Bunny, you got the right to dump me. I went to hell—and for *what*? I had the world right here. It's you. I love you, but if you—I mean—if you have to—"

"Dean." Bunny's gaze was sad and tired. "I've had enough of hurt and hurting people tonight. Just...get up and be my girlfriend."

Dean stared, uncomprehending, and Bunny held out

her hands.

When she helped Dean to her feet, Bunny beamed, her smile a sunrise. Dean lost words; thoughts. She could only put her arm around Bunny's shoulders and let Bunny lead the way, her girlfriend somehow possessing a determination and strength greater than a fried vampire's. Dean's eyes hurt as tears welled, and she wiped at one swiftly before Bunny could see.

"Okay?" Bunny asked, as she put one foot before the other.

"Uh, yeah." Dean looked down at the upturned ground they stumbled across. During the fight, her face had probably caused at least one furrow.

"We're both wrecks." Bunny looked to the forest's edge as she helped Dean along. "We need rest. Goddess's temple is closest."

"Bunny…" Dean didn't think she had steel left for what remained needing to be said. She kept her gaze on the ground. "The…Fairer Than, she, uh, kissed me."

"What?" Bunny uttered. She stopped, and Dean looked at her. "What?" she repeated.

Bunny did not look mad—yet. She stared at Dean as if she didn't understand, a mix of shock and curiosity. Dean tried to meet her gaze. "It kinda just happened. Maybe a joke, on her part. But…now I get it. Her power." She remembered the sensual fire that flew down into her still lungs and beyond, lighting her undead being. She'd swallowed a mini-sun, one a vampire was supposed to burn up in.

"I'm so sorry, Bunny. All this time I *was* blaming you. For—for handling her alone. Because maybe she was…" *Better.* Dean's chin dropped. "But you chose me, and now I *know* what you had to face. I just don't know how you resisted something like that for so lon—"

Bunny took hold of Dean's face and kissed her.

The world flipped, a slow-motion somersault of their two bodies with mouths connected, and perhaps Dean was flat on the ground, and perhaps Bunny was the sky, and perhaps gravity had become non-existent and they were in the stars, spinning.

Bunny broke their kiss. Her hair fell against Dean's face.

"Now...who kissed you?" Bunny asked.

Dean snatched Bunny up in her arms, regaining her feet.

"BUNNY BAKER KISSED ME," she shouted.

⇌

—*kissed me*—

The cry echoed above the temple of the Goddess.

—*kissed me*—

The faint echo faded over the middle of the lake, reaching one person's ear. Fairer Than lay stomach down on a flat rock rising above the lake's surface. Soaked, she rested her chin in a hand. Between the forefinger and thumb of her free hand, she held up a candy heart.

It was one that had not melted with the rest from her plunge into the lake. It read:

Best Girl

Fairer Than stared at the words.

"Best girl in the world," she murmured.

Mugg fluttered into view. "Pshaw. There are *girls* in the world. None better or worse. And right here." He gestured to the lake.

The heads of water maidens rose in the water, surrounding Fairer Than's rock. They looked at her, expectant.

Fairer Than dropped the candy into the water, chin still in her hand. She stared sightlessly.

"Very well," she said. She snatched up the closest water maiden and kissed her. They fell into the lake. Fairer Than's weight sunk them down into the sucking dark.

The end.

Next: *Body Chase: The Fall of Fairer Than*

ELIZABETH WATASIN

CHARM SCHOOL
BODY
CHASE

Read more in
Charm School Graphique Vol 1
and
Charm School Digital No 1-9

More from Elizabeth:
The Wrecking Faerie: A Charm School Novella Vol1
Body Chase: A Charm School Novella Vol 3

The Dark Victorian: Risen Vol 1
The Dark Victorian: Bones Vol 2
Ice Demon: A Dark Victorian Penny Dread Vol 1
Medusa: A Dark Victorian Penny Dread Vol 2
Sundark: An Elle Black Penny Dread Vol 1
Poison Garden: An Elle Black Penny Dread Vol 2
Monster Stalker: A Darquepunk Novel Vol 1
Bloody Nike: A Darquepunk Novel Vol 2

Author's Notes

Charm School, the comic book:

Charm School the comic book was originally published by Slave Labor Graphics (SLG Publishing) from 1999 to 2003. Written and drawn by me, there were nine issues, with a tenth and final issue long promised. Bunny first appeared in the comic book short story, *Bunny the Good Li'l Teen Witch*, published in *Action Girl Comics* #13 in 1997, also by SLG Publishing.

This novelization of the second *Charm School* story arc, *Hot Roddin' to Hell and Back!*, completes comic book issues #4 through #10. #10 was never published and as I write this, remains in thumbnail rough form, still ready for final pencils and inking. For many *Charm School* readers, that marks about fifteen years of waiting for the conclusion.

Additional comments:

Long time *Charm School* comic book readers would know that the *Hot Roddin' to Hell* was done in the spirit of Shakespeare's *Midsummer Night's Dream*.

Comic book readers would also know that the black and white art of *Charm School* was inspired by three works: *Love and Rockets* by Los Bros Hernandez (specifically Jaime Hernandez), *Betty & Veronica* by Dan DeCarlo, and finally, by Walt Kelly's *Pogo*. Any swamp scenes or interactions between Pippita and Fairer Than was in homage to Pogo'esque patois and settings.

Pippita addresses Fairer Than by a variety of famous (or notorious) male lovers' names, one being Leander, from the myth of Hero and Leander.

About The Author

Elizabeth Watasin is the author of the Gothic steampunk series *The Dark Victorian*, The *Elle Black Penny Dreads*, the *Darquepunk* series, and the creator/artist of the indie comics series *Charm School*, which was nominated for a Gaylactic Spectrum Award. A twenty year veteran of animation and comics, her credits include thirteen feature films, such as *Beauty and the Beast, Aladdin, The Lion King*, and *The Princess and the Frog*, and writing for *Disney Adventures* magazine. She lives in Los Angeles with her black cat named Draw, busy bringing readers uncanny heroines in shilling shockers, preternatural fantasies, and adventuress tales.

Sign up for the mailing list at A-Girl Studio.
www.a-girlstudio.com
amazon.com/author/elizabethwatasin
www.facebook.com/ElizabethWatasinX
twitter.com/ewatasin

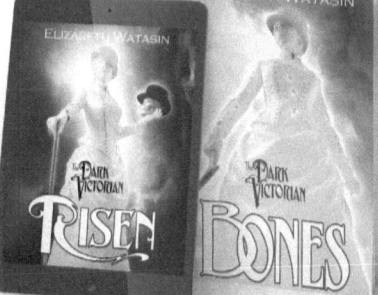

ELIZABETH WATASIN

The DARK
VICTORIAN

BONES